Readers love
ANDREW GREY

Fire and Flint

"…my sincere recommendation to anyone looking for a completely fresh story. You'll not regret picking this one up!"

—Divine Magazine

"I cannot recommend this enough. I loved it start to finish and while it had some super sweet, it was hot too. So grab your copy and enjoy!"

—Mistress Anya's Reading Nook

Heart Unheard

"This was an incredible book about learning to deal with a disability that one never expects to have to deal with."

—Gay Book Reviews

"So, if you like Andrew Grey's previous works, or are just looking for a great book involving two men who have to overcome a lot in life to get their happy-ever-after, then *Heart Unheard* might be the book for you."

—Top 2 Bottom Reviews

Taming the Beast

"I have no hesitation in recommending *Taming the Beast* to everyone who enjoys reading m/m romance stories."

—Love Bytes

"I have always liked the way Andrew Grey writes. He has a way of writing a gentle story that has a powerful message."

—Open Skye Book Reviews

By ANDREW GREY

Accompanied by a Waltz
Between Loathing and Love
Buried Passions
Chasing the Dream
Crossing Divides
Dominant Chord
Dutch Treat
Eastern Cowboy
In Search of a Story
Noble Intentions
North to the Future
One Good Deed
Path Not Taken
The Playmaker
Running to You
Saving Faithless Creek
Shared Revelations
Taming the Beast
Three Fates (Multiple Author
Anthology)
To Have, Hold, and Let Go
Turning the Page
Whipped Cream

ART
Legal Artistry • Artistic Appeal
Artistic Pursuits • Legal Tender

BOTTLED UP
The Best Revenge • Bottled Up
Uncorked • An Unexpected Vintage

BRONCO'S BOYS
Inside Out • Upside Down
Backward • Round and Round

THE BULLRIDERS
A Wild Ride • A Daring Ride
A Courageous Ride

BY FIRE
Redemption by Fire
Strengthened by Fire
Burnished by Fire • Heat Under Fire

CARLISLE COPS
Fire and Water • Fire and Ice
Fire and Rain • Fire and Snow
Fire and Hail • Fire and Fog

CARLISLE DEPUTIES
Fire and Flint

CHEMISTRY
Organic Chemistry • Biochemistry
Electrochemistry
Chemistry (Print Only Anthology)

DREAMSPUN DESIRES
#4 – The Lone Rancher
#28 – Poppy's Secret
#60 – The Best Worst Honeymoon Ever

EYES OF LOVE
Eyes Only for Me • Eyes Only for You

FOREVER YOURS
Can't Live Without You
Never Let You Go

GOOD FIGHT
The Good Fight • The Fight Within
The Fight for Identity
Takoda and Horse

Published by DREAMSPINNER PRESS
www.dreamspinnerpress.com

By ANDREW GREY

Published by DREAMSPINNER PRESS
www.dreamspinnerpress.com

RUNNING
TO YOU

ANDREW GREY

Published by

DREAMSPINNER PRESS

5032 Capital Circle SW, Suite 2, PMB# 279, Tallahassee, FL 32305-7886 USA
www.dreamspinnerpress.com

This is a work of fiction. Names, characters, places, and incidents either are the product of author imagination or are used fictitiously, and any resemblance to actual persons, living or dead, business establishments, events, or locales is entirely coincidental.

Running to You
© 2018 Andrew Grey.

Cover Art
© 2018 Kanaxa.
Cover content is for illustrative purposes only and any person depicted on the cover is a model.

Trade Paperback ISBN: 978-1-64080-570-5
Digital ISBN: 978-1-64080-413-5
Library of Congress Control Number: 2017919800
Trade Paperback published March 2018
v. 1.0

Printed in the United States of America
∞
This paper meets the requirements of
ANSI/NISO Z39.48-1992 (Permanence of Paper).

To Dominic, because he does everything he can to support me.

CHAPTER 1

BILLY JOE didn't move as he realized that being here was a huge mistake. He blanched and was relieved no one could see him. The chirping of birds and singing of cicadas had faded, replaced with a chorus of crickets emanating from the tall trees. Spanish moss hung from the branches, and the only light came from a bonfire that did little to pierce the blackness. The night was hot and sultry, but cold fear left Billy Joe with ice water running through his veins, wishing to hell he'd stayed home and kept his curiosity in check.

He turned and slowly made his way back down the old trail, hoping like hell he didn't step on anything. He made it about halfway to his car before his stomach rebelled, and he leaned over, losing his dinner in the undergrowth by the side of the trail.

He did his best to make as little sound as possible, wiped his lips, and continued on to the road. He stumbled to his old black Escape and got inside, started the engine, and pulled out, waiting for some distance to turn his lights on, hoping he was far enough away to not draw anyone's notice.

"Jesus Christ," Billy Joe breathed under his breath, gripping the wheel until his knuckles turned white, pressing the accelerator damn near to the floor in a desperate need to get the hell out of there. More than anything, he wished he could unsee what he'd witnessed. The reverend always said things happened for a reason. Billy Joe wondered if the long-winded old gasbag wasn't right about something for once, but he'd be damned if he could see the reason behind something like this.

Billy Joe's hands trembled, and he pulled off to the side of the road, breathing deeply, willing the shuddering in his hands and legs to subside. Damn it all, he wasn't going to do this again. He shook his hands rapidly and took calming breaths, pushing away what he'd seen. Billy Joe knew he had to seem as normal and relaxed as possible when he got back home. Feeling a little better, he got back onto the road, heading toward the city.

A plan—he needed a plan, Billy Joe realized as he reached the outskirts of town. He turned into a Walmart parking lot and hurried inside. Reaching an ATM, he used his card to take out as much cash as it would allow and stuffed it into his wallet. He grabbed a cart and decided now was a good time to do some shopping. Originally he'd thought that bringing a few things home might provide a cover for where he'd been, but as the image of his new future solidified, Billy Joe knew what he needed to do.

After trips up one aisle and down the next, he had the cart pretty full. Lastly, he added a couple of bags of chips and the Cheetos his mother adored to the top of the cart and headed for the checkout. He shifted his weight from foot to foot as he paid for everything, then pushed the cart out the door and to his car. He loaded everything into the back, out of sight, except for a single bag with the snacks, and drove home.

"Hi, Mama," Billy Joe said quietly as he stepped inside through the screen door. He set his bag on the table and hugged her the way he usually did, feeling very little. The scales had fallen from his eyes and he saw things more clearly. "How is Tyler? Thank you for watching him for me." He pulled out the chair and sat down, his balance going a little wonky.

"Were you drinking with those good-for-nothing friends of yours?" she scolded in a tone only mothers seem to have mastered— that weird mix of anger at the behavior and acceptance that boys will be boys.

"I stopped and had a beer at the Road House." That place was always so crowded that, on any given night, anyone could be there and no one was going to remember shit. "Only one, and then I got some snacks and came home. I needed a chance to breathe a little bit." Billy Joe pulled out the bag of snacks as a silent peace offering, at least to the tiny niggle of his conscience. He'd just lied to his mother, something he rarely did.

"It's all right. Tyler and I had a quiet evening, and he went to bed a couple hours ago. He's such an angel." She poured herself a mug of coffee and sat back down. She opened the bag of cheesy snacks and ate them one at a time. He knew from experience that she'd finish the entire bag if she allowed herself. But she closed the bag and put it away after a few minutes, the packaging rustling as Billy Joe left the room.

He quietly crept down the hall to Tyler's tiny room and peeked inside at his sleeping son. The space was little more than a closet that held Tyler's crib and small dresser. Billy Joe went inside and closed the door behind him. He stood next to the crib, watching Tyler sleep as a tear ran down his cheek, followed by another. He wiped them away, knowing they couldn't be seen, no matter what.

Tyler was the light of his life—an accident that had resulted in the greatest happiness and pride so far in his young life. Carol Ann had been the mistake. Getting involved with her had been hell. She'd said she was on the pill, but she'd lied or done something wrong. She got pregnant and had asked Billy Joe to take her out of state to a clinic so she could take care of it. When he'd refused, she threatened him, saying her father would come after him unless he agreed to marry her. At least he'd been smarter than that. He was not going to get trapped in a marriage with a girl who was involved with two other guys. In the end she had the baby, and he requested a paternity test. By some miracle, he was Tyler's father and agreed to raise him. Carol Ann was happy enough to sign whatever he wanted and walk away.

Tyler had blue eyes and light hair, gifts from his mother, and an easy disposition, from Billy Joe, according to his mother. Tyler sniffled and turned over, pulling at the blankets that Billy Joe had straightened. He settled down again immediately.

Billy Joe's plan solidified as he stood next to the crib, watching. He went to the window, looked out, and then glanced around the room. A clothes basket sat next to the dresser, with Tyler's folded laundry.

Billy Joe leaned over the side of the crib, kissed Tyler's hair gently, and picked up the basket. He opened the door, listened, and heard his mother still in the kitchen. Quietly, he went to his room, closed the door, and turned on the lights. He set the basket on the bed and hurried to the window. His father wasn't home yet. Billy Joe had to get busy.

He pulled open the closet door and shifted the junk of twenty-three years collected in the same place. "There has to be that old…." He smiled when he found the duffel bag and backpack he'd used when he'd gone camping in high school, in the back of the closet under a pile of old shoes. Billy Joe dusted them off and, as carefully as he could, emptied the contents of the laundry basket into the duffel. He gathered some of Tyler's books and stuffed toys, adding them to the bag, along with more clothes he had in one of his drawers because Tyler's little dresser was too small to hold everything. With the duffel full, he zipped it closed and stuffed it under the bed, out of sight.

Billy Joe cracked the door open. The flicker of the television lit the walls, the muffled volume on low, and he realized his mother was in the living room.

He closed the door and searched for something else to hold stuff. Getting down on his hands and knees, he checked under the bed, hoping for a box. An old suitcase caught his eye, and he tugged it out. It was small, with Chewbacca on it, and Billy Joe remembered using it when he was a kid. It must have been there for years, shoved back near the wall behind the leg of the bed. He filled it with more of Tyler's things and slid it back under the bed.

That part done, he needed something else. Maybe plastic garbage bags? He wished he'd thought to buy some at Walmart.

Billy Joe left his room, checking that everything looked normal. He grabbed the basket, took it back to the laundry area, and placed it with the others before joining his mother, who was slouched in the old recliner that no longer reclined.

"Where's Dad?" he asked as innocently as he dared.

"He went to a meeting." She popped a single Cheeto into her mouth, then licked the cheese off her fingers. "You shouldn't bring me these. I'll just eat them all." Her sigh filled the room. She got up, closed the bag once again, and put it in the kitchen cupboard with a soft bang. She returned and sat in the chair. She was getting older, her dark auburn hair now streaked with gray. She had been beautiful when she was younger, and vestiges of that beauty were still there. She took reasonable care of herself, in most ways.

"Did he say what he was doing?" Billy Joe pressed.

She shook her head, already turning her attention to one of the *Real Housewives* shows, with their manufactured, petty dramas. "He said there was someone they needed to teach a lesson." She didn't look at him until a commercial came on. "People like that need to learn their place, and it ain't around decent folks." The sharp snap in her voice told him all he needed to know. His mother was well aware of what was going on. "Now, let me watch my show." The ice in her tea tinkled as she lifted it to her lips.

Billy Joe sat with her a few minutes, knowing she wasn't going to be moving for a while. Then he got up and went down the hall to his parents' room. Billy Joe knew his mother kept a suitcase under the bed, and he dropped down, found it on her side, and pulled it out. He quietly returned to his room.

After closing the door, he opened the suitcase on the bed and began tossing in clothes from his dresser. He filled the backpack, added the important papers he kept in his top drawer, and then turned to the suitcase. Once it was bulging, he slid both it and the backpack under the bed.

"Daddy," Tyler cried, and Billy Joe glanced back to make sure the room appeared normal before going to Tyler's room.

Light briefly shone in the window and then faded. Billy Joe lifted Tyler into his arms, cradling him as he looked out the window in time to see his father's bulky silhouette lumber up the walk. "Is Grampy home?"

"I think so." Billy Joe grabbed the changing pad off the top of the dresser and got Tyler's diaper off, cleaned him up, and put him back in his pajamas. He wrapped up the wet diaper and placed it in a plastic bag to take out with him, then picked Tyler up again. "Go on back to sleep now."

"Is Grampy gonna yell?" Tyler hugged him tightly.

Billy Joe slowly rocked on his feet to lull Tyler back to sleep. "No yelling." He hoped. His father didn't talk; he barked and growled. "Just go back to sleep. I'm here, and it's nice and quiet."

The door opened and his father peered in. Billy Joe pretended not to notice and continued rocking Tyler, humming until he fell back to sleep and his father closed the door behind him. Billy Joe put Tyler in his crib and covered him with a light blanket in the air-conditioned room. He spied the diaper bag and filled it with additional clothes and supplies, stuffing the thing to the gills. He quietly left, intending to go back to his room.

"Boy," his father growled.

"Clyde, Tyler is asleep," his mother hushed gently.

His father flashed her a look of annoyance and turned to lead him out to the back screened-in porch. Billy Joe's blood ran colder with each step. "I need you to go to the construction office and open up in the morning. Just stay there and answer the phones until I come in." He glared, the stench of stale sweat and God knew what else rolling off him, along with high testosterone fueled by adrenaline. "I have some things I need to dispose of first thing."

Billy Joe nodded. "Sure. I can do that. But I have to go to work at noon." He tried to keep his voice light and carefree. He had to push what he'd seen out of his head, or standing this close to his father would make him sick.

His father pointed a finger at him menacingly. "Just do what I tell you and stay until I get back. If anyone asks, I'm at a job site. Left in the morning, and I'm expected back any time. You hear me, boy?" He curled his upper lip. "If anyone presses you, call me." He turned away and stomped back into the house.

Billy Joe followed. He went straight through to his room, closed the door, and lay on the bed. If the past replayed, his father would stay up for a while to calm down, and then his parents would go to bed. Thankfully they were both pretty heavy sleepers. He just needed to wait until they were asleep.

Billy Joe didn't dare move or draw attention to himself. He turned out his light and stared up at the ceiling. He had plenty of time to think on how much he hated his life here. His father was a bastard and a bully. His mother was kind enough but went along with his father. Hell, the two of them shared one mind on a lot of things. Billy Joe could take all that—they were his family, after all—but he didn't want Tyler growing up the way he had. He should have more than what they had here.

Tyler's wariness of his grampy truly sucked. But Billy Joe knew exactly how that felt. He had been taught to fear and obey the man from a young age. His father was only replicating the situation with his grandson. Tyler deserved better than that, and it was now up to Billy Joe to make sure his son had that chance. Getting the hell out of here was the only way it would happen. He'd known that for a while. Billy Joe began to shake as he remembered what he'd seen. Getting them both away wasn't a choice any longer.

Billy Joe listened as his parents headed to their room. All he needed to do was wait until they were asleep. He closed his eyes for a moment, then pulled the pillow up around his head as a rhythmic squeak from the next room reached his ears. God, that was the last thing he wanted to hear. He did not want to think of his parents going at it. They grew quiet quickly, and Billy Joe hoped to hell they fell to sleep fast as well.

Billy Joe dozed off and woke with a start. He got up and opened his bedroom door. The house was silent. He closed the door and opened his window. The heat and humidity rampaged into the room, but he ignored it. As silently as he could, he pulled the duffel bag and backpack out from under the bed and tossed them out the window. The small suitcase fit as well, and he pushed that out, watching as it landed in the grass. Billy Joe closed the window again, the air-conditioning working to banish the unseasonal heat.

He opened the door again and set the large suitcase just outside, then walked to Tyler's room as softly as he could so the damn floor didn't creak. He figured he was only going to get one chance at this. Once inside, he closed the door and gathered the two cases of diapers from under the changing table and tossed them out Tyler's window. Next he carefully lifted Tyler into his arms. Tyler fussed for a second and then fell to sleep on his shoulder. Billy Joe grabbed the diaper bag and slung it over his other shoulder. Then he left the room and returned to his, wishing he'd brought the suitcase with him. He retrieved it and carefully, step by step, headed for the front door.

He fiddled with the screen door. The damn thing stuck, and he had to work it open carefully to avoid the screech the fucking thing usually made.

Somehow, luck was with him, or maybe it was the humidity smoothing the way, but he made it outside and closed the screen most of the way before hurrying over the weedy lawn to his car. He opened the back door and got Tyler into his car seat, then wrestled the suitcase and diaper bag onto the driver's side of the back seat. He tiptoed over the yard and returned with the duffel and backpack. After he stowed the duffel in the trunk and the pack in the back seat, the second suitcase and diapers went in next. Billy Joe felt like a thief in the night, but he had to get the hell out of here, and the farther he could get before he was found out, the better.

The car was stuffed by the time he got in. Their house was at the top of a small rise, so Billy Joe put the car in neutral and rolled it forward onto the street. He let it pick up speed and started it once he was two houses away. The engine on the old thing came to life, and he sped away into the night.

BILLY JOE stopped at an ATM and withdrew more cash. If it wasn't the middle of the night, he'd have gone into a bank to take out what he had, but this was going to have to do for now. Hitting the highway, he headed north. Jackson disappeared in the rearview mirror, and he kept driving, the miles to Memphis ticking down. As he approached the city, he found a hotel and got Tyler out of the car. He needed to sleep, and Tyler needed to eat and play.

They napped in the hotel room, played a bit, and then once Tyler settled down for the night again, Billy Joe checked out and continued driving. All he was interested in was putting as much distance between him and Jackson as he could.

AT A rest area, while Tyler napped in his seat, Billy Joe stood outside the car. He found the Jackson police tip line number, breathed deeply to calm his racing heart, and made a call. The man who answered sounded impatient. Billy Joe tried to explain what he'd seen, but his words were jumbled and tripped over one another, and his nerves returned in force. He felt like a fool. He didn't sound coherent, even to himself. And when the officer asked if he'd been drinking, Billy Joe disconnected and leaned against the car, hanging his head. At least he'd tried.

It took a few minutes before he felt able to drive again, and then he got back in the car.

Billy Joe kept his phone off. He was sure his mother and father would try to call, and his phone was on their account, so they could track him if he turned it on. He smashed it to bits outside of Nashville and tossed the pieces in the trash, then bought a pay-as-you-go phone at Walmart.

Billy Joe figured the best direction to head was north and east, so he crossed the rest of Tennessee to Knoxville and then went north.

"Daddy, I'n hungry," Tyler said from the back seat.

"Okay, buddy. We'll get some dinner and then find a hotel where we can sleep." Billy Joe had been up for many more hours than he should have been and was bone-weary. A good night's sleep would do wonders. So after stopping at McDonalds for nuggets for Tyler, he found a budget hotel and an ATM for more cash.

He spotted a branch of his bank, so the next morning he went inside and emptied his checking account, in cash. The bank teller probably thought he was crazy, but Billy Joe didn't care. He brought the cash to the car and took off again.

Tyler was getting restless and fussy, which wasn't surprising since he'd been mostly in the car for two days. Billy Joe made sure to stop at roadside parks so Tyler could run and wear himself out. When he got another hotel, they had dinner and he played with Tyler, finally starting to relax. He was many hundreds of miles from home. While Tyler relaxed, Billy Joe collected all the cash he'd gotten together, placed it in one of the plastic grocery bags, and then slid it in one of the pockets of the suitcase and zipped it closed.

He fed Tyler a snack and then got him ready for bed. Lying there with Tyler in his arms, Billy Joe fell to sleep.

THE FARTHER they went, the looser Billy Joe's grip on the steering wheel got. For now he had plenty of money, and he hoped he'd be able to get a job somewhere and start a new life for Tyler. They continued north, the landscape growing bleaker and much less green. They passed through northern Virginia and then parts of West Virginia and Maryland, and then encountered snow. The temperature had dropped, but the car was warm. Billy Joe knew he was going to have to find a place to get some warmer clothes.

As they passed into Pennsylvania, the snow began coming down faster. The day was growing to an end, the light fading fast. He checked the map at a rest area and intended to make it to Harrisburg before stopping. It was maybe an hour away, and he knew he'd be able to find a place to stay. Tyler was hungry, so Billy Joe passed him a few crackers and a bottle with a little juice inside, and kept going.

The snow grew thicker, reminding Billy Joe of how unfamiliar he was with driving on roads like this. At home, the few times it had snowed, everyone just stayed inside until the sun melted it away again and then went on with their business. This snow didn't seem like it was going to behave that way.

He saw the sign for Shippensburg and got off the highway, traveling very slowly. He drove into a business area and pulled into the Walmart parking lot. Billy Joe wrapped Tyler in a blanket and carried him into the store, where he found the section for winter wear and bought them each a warm coat. Then he got them something to eat, and they returned to the car. He made it back to the freeway, intending to continue the last little bit for the night, but the car lurched and then cut out.

Billy Joe coasted to the side of the road and pulled to a stop as all the lights inside the car went dark. The wipers stopped and snow built up on the windshield and back window, the cold creeping in as the heater ceased blowing.

"I'n cold," Tyler said after a few minutes.

"I know, honey." He got the blanket and put it over him, trying to figure out what to do. He needed to get help and had his phone, but who did he call? Billy Joe was well away from anyone he might know, which was good and bad. He didn't want to call the auto club in case his parents could trace him. He was just about to give up and call anyway when headlights appeared behind him, coming to a stop.

CHAPTER 2

CARLOS MIRAS pulled to a stop behind the black Escape by the side of the highway. His father would probably tell him he was a fool, and his mother would probably say he had a good heart—too good a heart. But neither of their opinions mattered anymore. He was no longer part of their family. Carlos looked out his front window, wipers swishing back and forth to ward off the snow. He saw hints of light coming from inside the car, most likely from a cell phone.

He got out, pulling his coat closed around him. Carlos's hazard lights blinked red against the snow. He tapped on the window of the back door because he thought he saw movement. "Are you all right?" he shouted.

The back door opened to a man leaning over the back seat to a small child still in his car seat, covered in a blanket. "The car died, and I was trying to get him warm." The man turned and pulled back, eyes widening. Carlos had trouble placing the expression. "We'll be fine as soon as I call for help."

"Pop the hood. Let me take a look at it." Carlos had spent numerous hours working on cars with his father and brothers. Not that he'd been particularly into cars at the time, but he picked things up by osmosis. He went around to the front, and when the hood popped, he pushed it open and used his phone to illuminate the engine.

"It just went dark all of a sudden and everything stopped working," the man said, pulling himself into a coat after closing the car door.

Carlos bent over the engine and quickly found the problem. "It's the electrical system." He reconnected the main circuit to the alternator and stood back up. The hood light came on as though he'd flipped a switch, and Carlos closed the hood. "That ought to do it. I suggest you take it in to have it looked at, but you were pretty lucky."

The man turned the key, and the engine came to life. "Thanks," he said softly. "I was trying to make Harrisburg to get a hotel and…."

Carlos shook his head. "I don't think so. The snow isn't going to stop, and the roads are only going to get worse. I'd say to get a hotel, but with this weather, they have been reporting that almost everything is full." He sighed. "Let me make a call." He pulled out his phone and called his landlady, Mrs. Carmichael, and explained the situation. "I know it's unusual, but he has a little boy with him, and in this weather…."

She hummed a second. "The front place in your building is free. It's furnished, and they can stay there for the night," she offered.

"Thanks. I'll stop by and pick up the key from you and then make sure everything is okay in the morning." He hung up and turned to the other man. "I'm Carlos, by the way."

"Billy Joe," he said, keeping his hands shoved in his pockets. The plates on the car read Mississippi, so Carlos assumed he was as cold as Carlos had been when he'd first come this far north.

"My landlady has an apartment that's empty. You can use it for the night. It's furnished and will be warm. It's only one bedroom, but I bet you can make do." He came around the side as a few cars passed very slowly on the now-snow-covered freeway.

"Is it always like this?"

"No. This is a real early snow, but we can get them occasionally. I'll pass you, and you just follow me. I'll go slowly, as you'll need to be careful. It isn't far."

Carlos walked back to his car and waited so Billy Joe could get settled. Then Carlos pulled in front of him, and they drove slowly on the ever more treacherous road to the next exit and then down surface streets to his building. Carlos turned in and motioned Billy Joe to the parking spot next to his. Carlos got out and waited for Billy Joe, who got the little boy out of the back and followed him. Carlos knocked on Mrs. Carmichael's door.

She peered out and then opened her door. "Carlos," she said with a smile. "I have the key for you right here. It's the door just across the hall." She gazed around him, getting a look at Billy Joe.

"Don't worry, I'll get them settled." Carlos took the key and said good night, then led them up the stairs and unlocked the door. "Like I said, it's only one bedroom, but it should do for you for tonight, and at least you'll be warm. This snow should be over by the morning."

"Thank you," Billy Joe said softly as he went inside. "Is this okay, Tyler?" he asked, setting the boy down.

Tyler stood stock-still for a while. "I'm tired." He yawned, hurried to the sofa, and climbed onto it. Billy Joe turned on the television and found a program Tyler seemed to like.

"Do you want help bringing anything up?" Carlos asked.

Billy Joe shook his head, paling a little. "No. I can get it. But would you stay here with Tyler? I won't be long." Billy Joe hurried out and down the stairs. In no time, he raced back inside, weighted down by suitcases, a duffel, and a backpack, with a diaper bag around his neck. He looked like something out of an old Hollywood comedy sketch.

"Thank you for everything." Billy Joe seemed nervous, shifting his weight after setting everything down and looking around. Carlos's timing sucked, but Billy Joe's confusion and the way he bit his lower lip were adorable.

"You're welcome. I'm right across the hall if you need anything. Just knock in the morning so I can get the key back from you." Carlos went to leave the apartment, but stopped for a second, turning to where Billy Joe held his son tightly to him, fear in his eyes. It sent a chill up Carlos's back as he wondered about the source of it. He knew that fear, and the loneliness and mistrust that accompanied it. He'd lived that himself. It was as familiar as his brown eyes. Being rejected for who he was—a part of him he couldn't change—stayed with him and had become ingrained in the man he was now. "Is there anything more you need?"

Billy Joe shook his head, fear and pain rising in his eyes for some reason, so Carlos took his leave.

As soon as he closed the door behind him, Carlos realized Billy Joe was a little wary of him, from the tension in his stance, the way he took a step back when Carlos spoke, and the fact that he held his son more tightly and didn't turn away, his pupils wide. That didn't make any sense to Carlos. Yeah, Billy Joe didn't know him, but Carlos had helped him on the highway and gotten him a place to stay for the night. He could have driven by and just left them to their own devices. Besides, Carlos was the last person anyone should be afraid of. He was small and had never hurt anyone in his life. He'd been the one who was bullied growing up, not the bully.

Slightly confused but unable to do anything about the situation, he returned to his apartment. He had one of the two-bedroom units, which meant there was a small living room with a kitchen off to one side, as well as a hallway that led to a medium-sized bedroom and a tiny second bedroom that he used as an office of sorts.

When his phone buzzed in his pocket, Carlos answered it.

"Did you make it home okay?" Angie asked. They worked together, and with this weather, he should have known she'd check up on him. Angie was most definitely the mothering type, and Carlos loved her for it. Sometimes she carried it a little far, though.

"Yes. Have you left?" Angie was working the late shift at the library to handle a class that had come in.

"Not yet. I'm about to after this class finishes. How are the roads really?"

"Bad. Take it really careful and go slow. Hopefully the university is already plowing. But get out as soon as you can. It's really wet and sloppy. I passed cars on the side of the road, and helped one guy and his kid when their car broke down." He chuckled. "They're from Mississippi, judging by the plates, and he didn't know how to drive in this mess. He's lucky he didn't end up in the ditch or something."

Angie paused on the other side of the line. "What did you do?"

"I got the car going again, which was easy, and all the hotels are full, so—"

She inhaled sharply. It was an Angie trait. She was a drama queen of the highest order. "You didn't take him to your apartment, did you? You don't know anything about this guy and—"

"Angie," Carlos interrupted. "No, I didn't bring him to my apartment. He's in the one across the hall for the night. The guy has a toddler, and I wasn't going to let them freeze on a night like this if I was able to help." He spoke faster as he went on. "The kid, his name is Tyler. He was so cute, holding on to his dad in that little winter coat. What was I supposed to do?"

Angie clicked her tongue. "You're such a pushover. Maybe that's why we all love you."

Carlos chuckled. "Because I'm a pushover. Gee, thanks. That's good to know," he said, only partly joking.

"No. Because after all the crap you've been through, you still have a big heart. Just be careful with this guy. You don't know anything about him."

"It's only for one night. I don't know where he's heading, but that car was full to the brim. So, he isn't planning on returning to Mississippi any time soon." Carlos shrugged. "Be really careful going home and don't stay too late. The roads are only going to get worse."

"I promise I'll leave as soon as my class is done. I already closed up as much of the building as I can, so as soon as the students leave, I'll be out the door." She was her perky, almost chirpy self again. "Andy said he was going to cook something special for me." She practically hummed. Andy and Angie, they were an adorable couple.

"Awesome. Just text when you get home, and I'll see you tomorrow. This is supposed to stop sometime tonight." Carlos was about to hang up when Angie continued.

"I wanted to ask. Is the dad you helped cute?"

And here Carlos had thought he'd managed to escape Angie's matchmaking fanaticism… just once. She was the happiest person Carlos had ever known, and she wanted everyone to be as deliriously content as she was… whether they wanted it or not.

He groaned, trying to figure out how he could not answer without just hanging up.

Angie wasn't going to let it go. "Just tell me!"

"Dang it. Yeah, he was cute, in a sort of clueless, scared rabbit kind of way. The guy is running from something. That's pretty obvious, and there was fear written all over his face. I'm not sure what it was, but I think he looks the same way I did when I left Amarillo in the middle of the night. My cousin had threatened to kill me rather than have a *maricón* in his family." Carlos swallowed hard as he remembered packing and getting out of town ahead of the lynch mob.

"That bad?" She whistled softly. "Just be careful and don't get taken in."

He rolled his eyes. She was a total mother hen. "I'll be fine. It's only for a night, and tomorrow he'll probably be on his way." He ended the call, making her promise again to let him know when she made it home okay.

His stomach rumbled, reminding him he hadn't stopped to pick up something for dinner the way he originally had intended. He stared at the contents of his refrigerator and decided to reheat some pasta he'd made earlier in the week.

Carlos sat at his small table, eating his dinner. He was in no hurry, and a relaxing evening seemed in order. Once he was done, Carlos rinsed his dishes, headed to the sofa, and settled in to read.

Books were his passion, so he spent his spare time with them rather than the television. The wind rattled the windows, and even though the apartment was warm, the sound chilled him. He grabbed the blanket from off the back of the sofa and pulled it over him, making a nest before getting lost in the story of pirates and adventure on the high seas. Angie texted him that she was home just as he got back into the story.

CARLOS WOKE with the book on his chest and a slight crick in his back. He slowly got up, stretched, and checked the clock. It was well after midnight, so after marking his place, he set the book aside and trudged to the bathroom, where he got ready for bed.

He tried to remember the last time he'd had company. A couple of boyfriends in school and grad school, but none of them had really seemed to understand him. Their lives were all about cars, partying, and having fun. Jamie, his last boyfriend, had actually complained that Carlos was as serious as a heart attack and was too young to get that wound up about everything. Sure, Carlos liked to have fun, but his entire time in college and then grad school, he'd been about ten dollars away from going without food, with no parents or family helping him with his education or sending him a care package when things had gotten tight and he'd needed something extra to eat.

He pushed all that aside. It wasn't fruitful for him to go over it again. He had a job and was making his own way now. He needed to look forward, rather than into the past.

Still, it would be nice to have someone who thought the world revolved around him. He chuckled under his breath.

Carlos had just begun to doze off when he heard a knock on the front door and bolted upright in the bed. He got up, pulled on his robe, and trudged into the other room to peer out the peephole. He opened the door to find Billy Joe holding a blanket-wrapped Tyler.

"There's no heat…." Billy Joe shivered as he stepped inside. "I think it went out or something."

Carlos yawned. "Okay, let me take a look at it." He followed Billy Joe across the hall and stepped into the cold apartment. He found the thermostat, and it was set correctly, but nothing was happening. It was an older building, and thankfully Carlos knew where the electrical boxes were.

"I found the breakers in the hallway and couldn't find one that had been flipped," Billy Joe offered. He stayed at the other end of the room, well away from Carlos, clutching Tyler close. It seemed so strange. Carlos knew the fear that came with not being able to trust anyone, and this felt exactly like that to him. But what he didn't understand was why.

"Let me check one more thing." Carlos pulled open the utility closet and groaned, flipping the switch inside upward. The furnace flicked on and the fan started. Why anyone would put that kind of shutoff on the furnace was beyond him, but the builders of the place had done some crazy things. "I think that should do it." He checked the nearest register as hot air entered the room. "I had no idea about that."

"Thank you. Tyler was getting so cold, and I don't have the stuff for this kind of weather and…." Billy Joe held his son tighter, stroking his back through the blanket he had over him.

"No problem. I'm glad I could help. I don't want Tyler to get sick or anything." The room was warming, and Carlos needed to get back to bed. Whatever curiosity he had about Billy Joe was most likely not going to be answered, and it was none of his business anyway, regardless of how cute he was or lost he might seem. "I'll talk to you in the morning."

Carlos left, pulling the apartment door closed after him and walking across the hall. Carlos locked the apartment door and turned out the lights as he went, and climbed back into bed. He settled in for what was to turn out to be a restless night's sleep.

THE NEXT morning Carlos got up, dressed, and headed across the hall to see if he could hear anything inside. He definitely did and smiled as he knocked quietly. Rapid footsteps and giggles sounded on the other side of the door.

"Daddy!" The cry rang through the hall.

The door opened, and Billy Joe held a diapered little cherub. "Umm… we were just getting up and ready to go. I'm sorry if we're running late." Billy Joe stepped back, and Carlos did the same.

"The university is opening a couple hours late because of the weather, and I was going to make pancakes—"

"Cakes! Want cakes!" Tyler said with delight. "Cakes… cakes… cakes!" he sang.

"Ummm…." Billy Joe took another step back. "I don't want to be a problem. You've already done enough…." He rocked back and forth, and it was obvious Billy Joe wanted to close the door and put distance between them.

"Cakes. Daddy, cakes." Tyler squirmed to get down.

"I won't keep you." Carlos wasn't going to intrude where he wasn't wanted. Turning, he went back across the hall and into his apartment, figuring he still had to make something to eat for himself. He got out the ingredients and mixing bowl, and put a skillet on the stove.

A knock paused him in his task, and he opened the door to find Billy Joe standing outside.

"Cakes!" Tyler said enthusiastically.

"He really likes pancakes." Billy Joe had a slightly sleepy southern drawl that Carlos thought adorable.

"Then come in." Carlos motioned, and they stepped inside. Billy Joe looked all around and closed the door. "Why not have a seat? I'm just getting started. Can I get you some juice?" He hurried to the refrigerator and pulled out a bottle of OJ, then grabbed glasses and poured Billy Joe some, as well as himself. "Does Tyler drink milk?"

"Yeah," Billy Joe answered with a yawn and reached into the bag he'd brought with him. "I got a sippy cup for him."

Carlos poured some in and went back to making the batter, letting Billy Joe take care of the lid and stuff. "How long have you been on the road?" he asked. He didn't want to seem like he was prying, but he needed something to talk about. He tried not to keep looking back at Billy Joe but found it hard. His hair was dark, going every which way, and his nose a little crooked, probably from a break at some point.

"Three… no, four days now. We left Mississippi on Saturday morning."

"That's a long way." Carlos heated the pan and poured three small pancakes. Then he got out plates, silverware, and some butter and syrup, and placed them on the table. The batter had bubbled nicely, so he flipped the cakes, pleased with the color. "Where are you headed?"

"Not sure," Billy Joe answered. "Just had to get out."

That confirmed what Carlos thought, at least up to a point. "What about your family?"

Billy Joe seemed more nervous and didn't answer. Carlos didn't press.

"Do you want the first cakes?" Carlos asked Tyler.

Tyler got up and raced to the table. Billy Joe lifted him onto his lap, prepared Tyler's food, and helped to feed him. "Good?"

Tyler nodded with a smile. "Yummy."

"I had to get away from my family too." Carlos got the next batch started. "That was six years ago now. I don't talk to them at all. A cousin sent a card a while back, but nothing since."

"Is that… like a… cultural thing?" Billy Joe asked.

"No. It's a… my family is a bunch of—" He ground his teeth, censoring himself because of little ears. "My family is closed-minded and they didn't like me for… well… being me." Carlos poured another batch of small pancakes. He hadn't expected that his own resentment still simmered so hotly after all this time, but clearly he was still harboring more pain than he'd thought.

"We left before my family could discover... well, let's say that we left as a preemptive strike. I want to give Tyler a chance to grow up in a different and better atmosphere than the one I had." Billy Joe continued feeding a ravenous Tyler his breakfast.

"I know about things being bad at home," Carlos offered as another round of pancakes finished. He put them on a plate for Billy Joe. As much as he'd rejected his family, he still remembered the manners his mother drilled into him as a child. Carlos figured it was probably best to change the subject. "What sort of work do you do?"

"Construction." Billy Joe somehow juggled feeding Tyler and fixing a plate for himself. Carlos guessed that came with being a father. "I built houses and strip malls with my dad. I can do just about anything. I've done electrical and plumbing work. I finished up my training and was trying to get a spot on a crew doing electrical work so I could finish up and get a license. I'm good with my hands, I guess. I've hung drywall and done framing work. I even worked with stone guys and learned to make most repairs and stuff. I haven't figured out where I was going to stop, but getting a job is first once I figure it out." Billy Joe took a bite and fed one to Tyler.

"They're looking for people for the maintenance department at the university I work at. There were postings on the job boards for the last few weeks. You could apply there. The job comes with benefits, including insurance, dental, and even retirement. I don't know how the hours are or anything, but it's worth a try." Carlos poured another batch of pancakes as Tyler finished his. He certainly had an appetite. He made another small pancake for Tyler, and Tyler ate that one as well. Billy Joe kept Tyler on his lap as he ate the other two, and Carlos made some for himself.

"These are really good. Did your mom teach you how to make them?" Billy Joe ate quickly.

"No. Mom didn't think us boys should learn to cook. After I left and made my way to Pittsburgh for school, it was either learn to cook or starve. I didn't have any money to go out much. School cost money, and I was working all I could." Carlos stood straighter. "I paid my own way and now I'm a librarian here. It's a good place to work and they treat us pretty well."

Billy Joe nodded. "Do you think we could stay here? How much is the apartment?" He worked his fingers on the top of the table as though figuring what he had. "I didn't have any plans for where to stop. All I wanted was to get far enough away that Tyler and I could have a chance to start over."

"Well, this is pretty far from Mississippi." Carlos flipped the pancakes, got his own plate, and set it on the counter next to where he was working. "Do you want some more?" There was a little batter left. Billy Joe smiled and nodded. Carlos grabbed the pan, flipped the pancakes onto his plate, and made the final batch. The pan was hot enough that they didn't take long, and he turned off the flame and sat at the table. He passed a pancake to Billy Joe and buttered his stack.

"Yeah. I guess it is. Things are different here, and so much colder. I wasn't expecting that. Never been this far north before in my life." Billy Joe ate the pancake, and Carlos ate his breakfast.

"I think the place you're in is rented by the week, but we can talk to Mrs. Carmichael. I suppose a finished place is going to be easier for you to start with." It was pretty clear there was no furniture in that car. "If you want to get Tyler cleaned up, the bathroom is right over there, and we can go down and see what's available. These are nice places, but they aren't going to break the bank."

Billy Joe lifted Tyler and carried him off to the bathroom while Carlos checked the time. Then he rinsed the dishes and loaded the dishwasher.

Tyler raced back into the room and bounded to the sofa.

"Do you want to come in to the university and apply for a maintenance job? I can make a call so they see you if you want. I know one of the guys on the staff. He helps us in the library quite a bit." Carlos got his coat out of the closet and draped it over the chair. He checked outside. The sun had come out and the snow was already melting. The pavement was wet where it had been plowed, but it was definitely drivable.

"Why are you helping me?" Billy Joe asked. "I only met you last night, and you've done all this and...." His gaze narrowed. "What do you want from us?" The question came out as an accusation.

"Who said I wanted anything? I know what it feels like to be on your own for the first time, wondering if your family is after you or not." That was a bit of a stretch, but from Billy Joe's sharp intake of breath, Carlos had hit the mark. "It doesn't cost me anything to help you, and there's nothing I want in return." He widened his eyes at Billy Joe. "What kind of life have you led that an act of kindness is met with this kind of suspicion?"

"Not a very good one, I'm afraid." Which made sense, with the whole wanting to get the hell away.

"If you're interested in trying to get a job...." Carlos hurried to his office and returned with a map. "We're here right now, and this is the library where I work. I have a full morning, but after lunch, if you come in, I'll make a few calls and then I can take you over to where you need to apply." He checked the time once more. "Mrs. Carmichael should be up by now, so if you want to talk to her, it's probably a good time."

"Yeah, I should." Billy Joe got Tyler and said goodbye, then carried him across the hall.

Somehow Carlos didn't expect to see Billy Joe later, but what he did if he stayed was his business. Carlos had tried to be helpful, and that was all he could do. The rest was up to Billy Joe.

Carlos hurried into the bathroom to finish getting ready and checked himself in the mirror, making sure he was set. He grabbed his coat, shrugged it on, and grabbed his keys. On his way out, he passed Mrs. C's door, where Billy Joe was speaking to her. They seemed to be getting along, so maybe she would rent him the vacant unit. Carlos waved and smiled as he passed, hurrying out before he was late.

"SO WHAT happened?" Angie asked as she rushed into Carlos's office and closed the door. With the snow delay, the shortened morning had been extra hectic, but thankfully it had quieted down. Carlos had been hoping to have a few minutes to catch up on email, but it looked like that wasn't going to happen. "I see he didn't sneak over and kill you in the middle of the night."

Carlos groaned as he stood, placing his hand on her forehead. "Are you delusional? Where would you get that idea? I helped him on the side of the road and got him a room for the night. That was all. And he might stop by today. He has construction skills, and they have been looking for people for maintenance."

She shook her head, tsking softly. "You just can't help it, can you?"

"What?" he asked with fake innocence. "I told him about the job, and if he comes by, I'll make a call to see if they'll talk to him. Nothing more." He narrowed his gaze. "Why am I explaining all this to you if you're just going to give me grief?" Carlos sat back down.

"Because I love you and don't want you getting hurt. Anything could have happened." She lowered herself into his guest chair. "You're a sweet guy—sometimes too sweet and kind for your own good."

Carlos snorted and placed his hand over his mouth. "I am not. The guy had a kid—I wasn't going to let them freeze." He leaned forward. "He's left his family to try to make a better life for his son. Does that sound at all familiar to you? It does to me. So, I'm giving him a little help." He crossed his arms over his chest.

"You like this guy," she pressed. "I can tell these things."

"Oh God. If I look at a guy for two seconds, you think I like him." Carlos's cheeks heated, and dammit, Angie smiled. "Okay, he's cute, like a lost puppy, but.... He's one of those guys who's had a hard life, yet when he does relax, the lines near his green eyes smooth out and...." He lowered his voice and let his arms fall to his sides again. "It's like he's scared of me or something. Me? I don't get it." There was nothing remotely intimidating about him in the least. He was a skinny, half-Mexican kid from Amarillo, the one who'd gotten stuffed into lockers for most of the time he was in high school.

Her expression softened. "Just be careful, okay? You don't know anything about him. So don't stick your neck out and give him a reference or anything. It's nice that you're willing to help— most people wouldn't." She patted his arm.

"Okay." Carlos put his hand up and leaned over the desk. "You and Andy really need to get a puppy, because this whole mothering thing is getting a little out of hand." He loved teasing her, and she smiled, her cheeks reddening.

Carlos's desk phone rang, and he broke away to answer it.

"Mr. Miras, there's someone out here asking for you."

"Thanks, Marie. I'll be out in a few minutes." He put the receiver back in the cradle. He checked the time, and Angie must have done the same thing. She waved and left the office. They had a staff meeting in fifteen minutes.

Carlos, relieved Angie didn't have time to ask about the call, left his office and headed through the building to the central reception area. Billy Joe and Tyler stood near the desk, looking all around, with Tyler pulling on his dad's hand.

"Billy Joe?" Carlos said gently, but Billy Joe still tensed and then relaxed some.

"I decided to try for the maintenance job." Billy Joe lifted Tyler into his arms. The tension rolling off Billy Joe was palpable, and Carlos had no idea why, but Billy Joe grew more and more rigid by the second.

"Good." Carlos checked his watch. "I have a staff meeting in less than ten minutes. I can take you over right after that, or if you'd like, I can see if one of the students can take you over now."

"I can wait," Billy Joe said and carried Tyler to one of the chairs.

"It's okay," Marie said, digging into her bag. She came up with a lollipop and asked if it was okay. When Billy Joe nodded reluctantly, watching as though it might have arsenic, Tyler raced over to her. "I'll help watch him." She came around her desk and knelt down, and Tyler took the sucker, laughing as he brought it back to Billy Joe, who kept watching Marie. Well, his caution was telling, and the little fantasies that had been playing in Carlos's head for much of the night and morning flew out the window.

CHAPTER 3

THINGS HERE were so very different. But maybe they weren't. Maybe things were like this in Mississippi too, but his family had warped and twisted their views to the point that Billy Joe was afraid of his own shadow half the fucking time.

Billy Joe took a deep breath as Marie, the nice older black lady from behind the desk, found a toy truck in the lost-and-found and gave it to Tyler to play with.

People here were nice. Carlos was nice.

He sat back in the uncomfortable seats. Tyler laughed as he sat on the floor, alternately playing with his car and doing peekaboo with Marie when she had a few minutes.

Back home, someone like Marie wouldn't have dared approach Tyler. Everyone knew Billy Joe, or at least they knew who his father was, and they would stay well clear of him at almost any cost. Marie, who didn't know Billy Joe's father, had been kind to him instead of afraid of him. Billy Joe knew he needed to adjust his thinking. He was no longer in the South, and he certainly wasn't in the neighborhood of Jackson where his family lived. Attitudes were different here, and that was why he'd left in the first place. He wanted Tyler to be free of the hate and bigotry that characterized his family, and that meant changing his own attitudes and preconceptions.

Which was probably going to be a lot easier said than done.

Billy Joe tried like hell not to be nervous and fidget the entire time he sat in the library, the kind of place he knew he had no business being in. He'd never be able to attend a college like this, and all the kids who passed through… they might not have noticed him, but he knew without a doubt that he was the dumbest one in the room—probably the building. It was intimidating as all shit, and he wished he could somehow disappear into the walls. If his father were in a situation like this, he'd lash out at someone, make a rude comment, or try to impose his stupidity on someone else in order to feel as though he were important. But Billy Joe just wanted to hide or leave.

"Sir." Marie's voice pulled him out of his thoughts. "Are you all right?"

Billy Joe nodded, realizing he'd been gripping the arms of the chair so tightly his hands had turned white and his arms were shaking. He released them and set his hands in his lap. "Sorry." God, he was a fucking mess. But for now, he and Tyler had a place to live, and he needed to be thankful for that. Now he just needed to get a job, and once he did, he could start to build a life here, away from….

His thought drifted away as Carlos strode toward him, his hips swaying slightly, a smile curling on his lips, his eyes as deep and dark as a cave, but one Billy Joe wanted to get lost in. He was slight in build, so the word "cute" came to mind, but Carlos was more than that. He was hot, with his rich, smooth skin, which slipped down into Carlos's open collar, and his jet-black hair that flowed almost to his shoulders. Carlos was more than enough to make him forget about his troublesome family. Hell, just watching him was enough to make Billy Joe forget about just about anything else.

"Are you ready to go?" Carlos asked, and Billy Joe got Tyler's things together, lifted him into his arms, and walked over to the desk to return the toy truck.

"It's okay. He can keep it. It's been here for months and we were just about to clean out the box." Marie's smile reached her eyes, and she tickled Tyler's belly, receiving a giggle that was music to Billy Joe's ears.

"Thank you," Billy Joe told her with a smile that he really felt. "That's very kind." He put the toy in the diaper bag and helped

Tyler get his coat on. Then he put on his own and lifted Tyler once again before joining Carlos.

"All ready?" Carlos asked, and after Billy Joe nodded, he turned to Marie. "If anyone needs me, I'll be back shortly." Carlos turned and led the way out the back door. "In the spring this entire area will be filled with flowers—daffodils, tulips—the area filled with color. It's my favorite time of year."

Billy Joe shivered as the wind rushed around him, the snow almost blinding in the bright sunshine. Tyler buried his face in Billy Joe's shoulder to shield his eyes as they walked across the campus. "Is it always this cold this time of year?" The sun was strong, the rays warming his coat even as the wind pulled the heat away.

"No. It's usually nicer, and this snow isn't going to last long. It will get warmer before winter settles in for good." Carlos pointed. "We're headed over this way." He turned and smiled. "I'm glad you decided to stay. This is a nice area, with good people."

Billy Joe nodded. He was already aware of that. "Me too."

Carlos stopped. "I forgot to ask, do you have all your paperwork? Social Security card, stuff like that? They're going to ask for it." He bit his lower lip. "Maybe we should have put together a résumé."

"There ain't much to put together. My work has almost all been for my father at his company, and I don't want anyone contacting him to say where I am." Billy Joe held Tyler closer, patting his back gently. Maybe this wasn't such a good idea after all.

"Don't worry," Carlos said, placing his hand on Billy Joe's shoulder. Billy Joe felt the heat through his coat and all the way down to his bones. He closed his eyes for just a second. "They won't call anyone you don't want them to. You can put down the experience but say they aren't to contact him and don't give them the information."

"But won't they want to talk to someone?" Billy Joe asked.

"References aren't what they once were." Carlos pointed again, and they headed in that direction.

Warmth surrounded them as soon as they entered a low, long, utilitarian building. Billy Joe set Tyler down and held his hand as they made their way through the hallways and down to a set of doors.

Carlos led them inside. "Don't worry. I already called the head of maintenance to put in a good word. They'll help you." He smiled, and Billy Joe stepped inside and up to the window to explain nervously why he was there.

BILLY JOE heard Carlos in the hallway outside, and he thought about opening the door to see how his day went and to find out if anyone had said anything to him about how Billy Joe had done. He'd never interviewed with anyone—well, at least strangers— before. Billy Joe had gotten all his previous jobs because of his father or through people he knew. Even in high school, when he'd worked at the mill on weekends, his supervisor was a man he knew through his extended family. Then after just barely graduating, he went to work for his father. Everyone knew him in their circle of friends, and they all had the same beliefs. That was how it worked back home.

A knock pulled him out of his thoughts. Billy Joe hurried to open the door as Tyler ran over.

"Hey." Carlos hugged Tyler, smiling up at Billy Joe. "How did the interview go?" Carlos asked.

Billy Joe tensed for a second, then shrugged. Carlos had been good to them. "I was hoping you'd tell me. I met with the lady from personnel and filled out a mess of forms. She's from Tupelo, so we talked a spell about things back home. We didn't know any of the same folks, but it was nice to hear someone talk like me, rather than you Yankees." He smiled, hoping he could lighten a mood that had been pressing in on him. He needed a job. He'd paid for a month's rent in advance and still had some money left, but he wasn't going to be able to take care of himself and Tyler for very long without an income.

Carlos chuckled. "I bet it does, gringo." He let his own accent slip in, and Billy Joe smiled as he held Tyler's hand.

"After that, the head of maintenance came in to talk to me, and I think we understand each other. He told me what he needed, and I explained all the things I had done back home. Every time he mentioned a skill, I told him about a job I'd done that proved I had it." Excitement built inside, and Billy Joe picked up Tyler. "Did he call you?"

Carlos shook his head. "I wouldn't expect him to. He has a side business restoring cars, so he and I talk techniques and engines when we get together. I'm glad he talked to you today. That can only mean that they'll arrive at a decision that much sooner." He tickled Tyler's belly. "I'm glad it went well, and I suspect they'll make a decision pretty soon, but it's out of my hands from here."

Billy Joe nodded. "You can open the door, but it's up to me to walk through." His grandpa had told him that before he died five years ago. It was the one decent thing the old fuck ever said to him.

"Something like that." Carlos glanced over his shoulder into his apartment, then turned back to them. "I'm going to make some pasta for dinner. Do you want to join me?"

"You don't have to feed us every meal," Billy Joe said, even as he smiled at Carlos's offer. "I stopped at the store on the way home and got some things. I don't cook very well, but I can make salad."

"Then bring some if you'd like." Carlos checked his watch. "In an hour. Is that good?"

Billy Joe agreed, and Carlos waved to Tyler and then said goodbye, closing the door as he left.

"He's nice," Tyler said before going back to playing with his cars.

Billy Joe had to agree. Carlos was very nice, and back home, he never would have met him or even considered speaking to him, for fear of retribution from his father. Now it seemed Billy Joe had difficulty keeping the dark-haired beauty with liquid chocolate eyes out of his thoughts.

He sat down on the old sofa. It had seen better days, but it was clean; Billy Joe had seen to that. Tyler climbed up next to him, and Billy Joe shifted him onto his lap. "You know, this might just turn out to be a good place for us. Right?"

Tyler nodded his agreement.

"If I get the job, then they have insurance and they offer day care. You can play with other kids while I'm at work." He smiled and held Tyler a little tighter. "And here we can be who we want to be." He'd thought about it on his way back from the university. No one knew them here. He didn't have to be Clyde Massier's son. He could just be Billy Joe, and he got to figure out who that was going to be. He didn't have to put on a front and pretend he was someone else.

There had been plenty of gay kids at the campus. It was obvious, and they were open. He'd seen one couple holding hands in the library on his way to his interview. God, he wanted that so badly. Billy Joe had watched them climb the steps, envying their happiness and closeness as they bumped each other in the wide stairs, smiling with delight in their eyes. It had taken Billy Joe a while to decide what the look meant; it was so foreign to him. In his world, people found delight by sneering at the expense of someone else, not in true, unabashed happiness.

"I can be the person I really am," Billy Joe said in a whisper.

"Daddy." Tyler squirmed, so Billy Joe let him get down and back to his toys on the floor.

"Sorry, Buddy," he said.

"Is Grampy going to come here?" Tyler asked.

"Do you want him to?" Billy Joe asked, more to get a reading on how Tyler felt about the fact that he wasn't going to be seeing his grandparents… or anyone from home again, if Billy Joe could help it.

Tyler shook his head. "Grampy is grumpy." He zoomed his car across the room, chasing after it as though he didn't have a care in the world. Sometimes Billy Joe would give anything to be able to go back to that kind of innocence.

He sat still, watching Tyler play happily until he remembered he was supposed to be making salad to take to Carlos's for dinner. Billy Joe jumped up and got busy, pulling out what he had. It was pretty simple stuff, but he added some cheese to the lettuce, tomato, and cucumbers, and wondered what else he could add. There wasn't much. Billy Joe ended up leaving the salad as it was and hoped Carlos had some dressing, because he'd forgotten to buy any. He was an awful shopper. That was something else he was going to have to learn. Billy Joe set the bowl to the side and took out the last unopened bag of chips to add to the things to take. It was pretty meager offerings, but all he had.

Tyler whined that he was hungry, so Billy Joe calmed him, got things together in the diaper bag, and gave Tyler the chips to carry before making the trek across the hall with the salad bowl.

"Come on in," Carlos called when Billy Joe knocked, and he opened the door. The tangy scent of tomato sauce, garlic, and herbs wound around him as he stepped inside.

"Mmm," Tyler said as he hurried inside, nearly falling on the bag of chips, but Billy Joe set the bowl on the table and managed to catch him before he crushed the bag completely.

"It's just about ready." Carlos got out bowls and glasses, as well as salad dressing. "This one is ranch, which I make myself. I hate the bottled stuff, and one of the restaurants I worked in when I was in college gave me this recipe. It's the best." He set an unlabeled mayonnaise jar on the table, its contents flecked with green herbs.

Billy Joe was wondering what he could do to help when he saw the booster seat at one of the places. He swallowed hard, realizing Carlos had set it up just for Tyler because he wanted them to be able to come over to eat. Thankfully Carlos was turned away, because Billy Joe didn't want him to see him fall to pieces. Dammit, Carlos was so nice and not at all what Billy Joe had heard about people like him his entire damn life. His dad talked about Mexicans as "lazy, good-for-nothing beggars" who should be sent across the border and shot if they tried to come back. Just more crap from his father that he never believed in the first place.

"Do you want to get up in your seat?" Billy Joe asked Tyler to cover the rise of emotions that he was having trouble controlling.

"Please do." Carlos dished up the pasta and set the bowls at their places. He put a dish towel around Tyler's neck, tying it in back. Then he placed a small plastic bowl of buttered pasta in front of Tyler, who picked up the pasta with his fingers and shoved it into his mouth. "I got his out first to let it cool."

Tyler certainly seemed happy, making yummy sounds.

Billy Joe waited for Carlos to join him and then took his first bite, the garlicky flavor of the sauce bursting on his tongue. It was stunning, and he ate faster, immediately hungry. "Wow, this is awesome."

Carlos took his. "Thanks. It did turn out pretty well."

"I'll say so." Billy Joe ate, savoring each bite. "I bet you make amazing Mexican food. I love it."

Carlos shook his head. "I don't cook Mexican food because my mother never taught me any of her dishes. I cook Italian and American food because that's what I learned working in restaurants and kitchens."

Billy Joe swallowed. "I guess I figured…." He lowered his gaze to the table. This new world he was trying to navigate was going to be harder than he expected. "Sorry. I remember now that you said your mom and dad didn't believe in you learning how to cook."

Carlos sighed. "I can make tacos, but that's about it. See, I don't have much to do with my family. They rejected me and cast me out, so eating Mexican food brings up bad memories. I basically turned my back on that part of my life. And when I make tacos, I do it from one of those kits in the grocery store." He took another bite.

Billy Joe supposed he couldn't really blame him. "Do you speak Spanish?"

"I spoke it at home with my grandparents. But I haven't used it a great deal since I left. Though at times being bilingual has helped at work." Carlos stabbed at his pasta.

Billy Joe rolled his eyes. "That sounds pretty dumb to me."

Carlos snapped his head up. "You're calling me dumb?" There was no humor in his expression, none whatsoever.

"No. But you can speak a different language. That's a skill, a skill that I wish I had. Now me, I speak two languages, English and what my family talks—moron." Billy Joe smiled, and Carlos rolled his eyes. "Well, maybe not moron. More like dipshit."

Carlos laughed. "You're killing me here. Come on…."

"Well, it makes as much sense as you not using a skill that could benefit you just to spite people who are over a thousand miles away. Who cares what they think? I drove all this way so I don't have to give a crap what my family thinks. You did the same." Sometimes things really made sense for him, and Billy Joe wished that happened more often. Often the rest of the world seemed to understand everything and he was left behind, on the outside. "I don't want them to control me or Tyler anymore."

Carlos picked up his water glass and held it there. Billy Joe raised his in return. "Here's to leaving useless families in the past and a thousand miles away." They clinked glasses.

"May they stay there," Billy Joe added as Tyler picked up his sippy cup, grinning, wanting to get in on the fun. They all touched cups and drank. Billy Joe was surprised at how the show of solidarity touched his heart. He'd actually met someone who understood to a degree what he'd gone through and how hard it was to simply walk away from everything and everyone he'd ever known. Being alone, utterly alone, with no safety net of any kind, was gut-wrenchingly terrifying. What the hell would happen if he failed? Going home to his family would be taking his life in his hands, and he had more than himself to worry about. He was doing this for Tyler, and he needed to somehow build a life for him. That was the most important thing.

"And not decide to turn up like a bad penny," Carlos added.

Billy Joe felt himself pale. The very thought was enough to send a ripple of ice up his back. "Does your family know where you are? I don't think mine has a clue, and I have to figure out how to keep it that way." He needed to get a new driver's license and register his car here. Get everything out of Mississippi and into Pennsylvania, where his family and his father's connections were going to have a harder time tracing him.

Carlos shook his head. "I don't think so. I've contacted a few of the more sympathetic family members a few times just to let them know I was still alive, but I haven't done that in a while and I usually do it by phone. My number is still the same, so when I call, it doesn't show anything other than a local number to them. I've never told anyone where I was living, but they knew I got a scholarship to Penn State, so I think they suspect I'm in this area of the country, but anything more detailed than that…."

"They could google you," Billy Joe offered.

Carlos nodded. "It's really difficult to hide nowdays. But there are lots of Carlos Mirases for them to sort through if they try. They haven't bothered contacting me, so I hope they don't try. I haven't given them any reason to, and it's fine with me. You, on the other hand…. Once you get a license, it will be part of the public record. The most important thing is that they aren't going to know which is you or what area of the country you're living in. It will be hard if they just search for your name, especially if you don't do anything newsworthy." Carlos grinned. "Mostly they're going to get those awful scam sites that try to sell you information on whoever you're looking for."

"My dad isn't savvy like that, and he's way too cheap to pay for something like that. Now, if he could get someone else to find out what he wants...." Billy Joe scratched the back of his head, thinking. His family would try to find him. His father couldn't have known he'd been approaching the gathering and had seen.... Billy Joe shivered. Every time he closed his eyes, he saw that scene played out again and again. Still, him disappearing when he did was going to make his father suspicious, and the fact that Billy Joe had taken Tyler with him.... "I wish I could say the same thing. My father... he holds tight to what he believes is his, and... I'm going to have to do all I can to stay out of sight."

"Then pay Mrs. C in cash and there wouldn't be checks. You should open a new bank account here and close the one you had back home, or leave a little in it and let it go dormant. What bank was it with?"

"First Bank of Mississippi."

"Then open an account at a national bank and transfer the money there," Carlos offered. "Once it's out, you could then transfer it somewhere else if you wanted. Confuse them if they tried to trace it."

Billy Joe wasn't sure if it was that easy, but he had to get access to the money he still had in savings eventually.

"Is your family on the accounts?" Carlos asked. "If they aren't, then they can't access the information."

Billy Joe sighed. "My dad knows everyone in town, so there's always someone at the bank... you know, the good old 'shit for brains and the law doesn't apply to them' network.... Well, he knows people at the bank, and all they have to do is look up the information and give it to my dad. Hell, they'd think they were doing a buddy a favor... stuff like that." Billy Joe needed time to think this over. It was more complicated than he'd thought it would be. The cash he had wasn't going to last him a whole lot longer if he didn't get a job, and even when he did, getting paid was going to take time.

He finished most of his pasta.

Carlos opened the chips, and Billy Joe put a few on Tyler's bowl, along with a few cucumbers from the salad. He tried some of Carlos's dressing, and man, that was good. Bottled stuff was never going to be the same again.

A phone rang, and Carlos pushed back his chair, excusing himself to go into the other room. He returned a few minutes later, smiling. "That was my friend in maintenance. Whatever you did, they were apparently impressed. He thanked me for sending you their way. So that's good. The powers that be need to make some decisions, though, and that will happen in its own time."

"Okay. So I need to be patient." Billy Joe tried not to get his hopes up. He figured he'd need to get out there and scout the area for other jobs in the next few days. Construction crews almost always needed people, and he could do a lot of different things.

"Sometimes that's the hardest part of the process." Carlos picked up the dirty dishes and took them to the sink. "I have some ice cream if you want some. I bet he does." He opened the freezer, got out a couple of containers, and set them on the table before getting bowls. "Help yourself." Carlos put a little vanilla in a dish and sat next to Tyler. "Do you want some?" He held up the spoon, and Tyler opened his mouth, letting Carlos feed him.

Able to relax for a little while, Billy Joe got a scoop of the chocolate and took a bite. It was nice that Carlos was willing to spend time with Tyler, and Tyler liked him.

"Is that good?" Billy Joe asked, taking his seat. Tyler nodded, watching Carlos's every move, opening his mouth like a baby bird whenever another spoonful of ice cream made an appearance.

Billy Joe finished his dish as Tyler did, and then Carlos put the ice cream away. "Aren't you having any?"

"I'm okay for now." Carlos helped Tyler down, wiped his face and hands on the dish towel, then let him play on the floor.

"Thank you for having us. It was very nice," Billy Joe said as he leaned back in his chair, stuffed to the gills. "You've been so helpful, and I don't know how to thank you. If it weren't for you, we'd probably still be sitting by the side of the road."

Billy Joe's gaze latched on to Carlos's backside, and he looked his fill while Carlos was turned away. He knew Carlos was gay—Carlos had told him as much already—but it still seemed strange to be looking outright. That sort of thing would never be tolerated by his family or anyone back home. It would be *the* cardinal sin and probably one that would put him in danger, so Billy Joe had taught himself not to look, to keep his head down and not look at other guys under any circumstances. Damn, but Carlos had a tight, perfect bubble butt and narrow hips. Nice legs too, and when he shifted his weight, those cheeks bounced and shifted under his pants.

Billy Joe crossed his legs and adjusted himself to hide the fact that he was already getting excited. That was a bad idea. He hadn't had many chances at any sort of intimacy in the last few years. He'd been too scared to allow himself that. God, he wanted to know what it would be like to hold hands with Carlos as they walked through the library the way those students had, or find out what he tasted like and how his lips felt against his. Billy Joe wanted to be able to touch, maybe find out how that perfect butt felt in his hands.

He closed his eyes, letting his imagination take flight for just a few seconds. There was no harm in a little wishing. Hell, in his entire life, his real hopes and dreams had been relegated to wishes he held deep in his heart, away from all prying eyes. It was the one place he knew they would be safe from everyone and wouldn't cause him hurt.

"I feel you watching me," Carlos said with a hint of mirth as he turned around.

Billy Joe blushed and turned away. "I think I should take Tyler home and put him to bed." Changing the subject was a good thing right about now. He wasn't ready to talk about his attraction to Carlos or what it meant. It had only been a few days since he'd left the viselike confines of his family, and there were only so many things he could change at one time. "Thank you so much for dinner. It was really nice." He gathered Tyler's things and then picked him up, realizing Tyler was in desperate need of a diaper change.

"You're welcome." Carlos wiped his hands and opened the apartment door. "Let me know when you hear something about the job." The heat in Carlos's eyes sent warmth racing through Billy Joe, but he wasn't ready to admit that yet, at least not out loud.

"I will, and thank you again." Billy Joe stood in the doorway, wondering how to properly say good night. Carlos came closer, their gazes meeting, and the air around him heated further. Billy Joe's head spun and he parted his lips, licking them slightly, unsure of what was going to happen next.

"Come over any time. It's nice having the two of you." Carlos smiled and gently placed a hand on Billy Joe's shoulder. "These feelings you're struggling with, trying to figure out who you are, are confusing for everyone. I went through them, and so do most people at some point in their life. When you're different from other people, you have to figure out your own road map. I had to do that after my family turned their backs on me. You have to do it now."

Billy Joe nodded. "But how?"

"We all have to take our own journey. Give yourself some time. Things are different here than they were back home. The people here are much more tolerant and supportive. It's doubtful that anyone is going to look down on you for being gay, or anything else you discover about yourself." Carlos lifted his hand off Billy Joe's shoulder and shifted it to his cheek. "I'm not an expert or anything. But I've been through it. I will tell you this: you're allowed to look at me all you want, and I'm not going to be insulted or...." Now Carlos blushed. "Actually, I think I'm flattered." Carlos closed the distance between them, pulled his hand away, and kissed him on the cheek. Billy Joe couldn't help touching his skin where Carlos's lips had been. "Good night."

Billy Joe stepped across the hall and went into his own apartment. He took care of Tyler, removing his diaper and bathing him, then got him ready for bed. He read Tyler a story and let him fall asleep. He returned to the living room and sat on the sofa to watch television. After all that time, he could still feel the residual heat from Carlos's kiss.

CHAPTER 4

IT HAD been an interesting week. Carlos went to work and went home each night to dinner, usually with Billy Joe and Tyler. Carlos loved cooking and pretty much expected that Billy Joe and Tyler would exist on microwave meals and junk food otherwise. It was nice having someone to spend some time with rather than sitting behind his computer, watching television, or reading for hours, alone. What surprised him most was how easily he fell into that routine.

"Carlos," Billy Joe called as Carlos climbed the stairs, carrying bags from the grocery store. Billy Joe raced down, took some from him, and hauled them up. Tyler waited at the top of the stairs, a stuffed horse that Carlos had found when he was going through a box of his old things tucked under his arm. "I got a call. They want me to start on Monday. I have to fill out paperwork and things like that, and then they'll show me the ropes." Billy Joe grinned from ear to ear. "When I told the lady from personnel that I needed childcare, she referred me to the on-campus day care. They apparently have staff who work with students majoring in child development to run the place. She said her daughter goes there." Billy Joe seemed so excited, he was about to burst.

"That's awesome. Be sure to ask how much the day care costs so you can work that into your budget. I've heard that it's very reasonable for students and staff." Carlos had been helping Billy Joe with a plan for his money so he knew what to expect and could meet his regular monthly expenses.

Billy Joe's scent tickled Carlos's nose, and Carlos inhaled softly to take in his rich, musky scent, letting it work its tingly magic all the way down to his toes. "They're paying me well too.

More than I made back home." Billy Joe grinned. At least with the job and the apartment, he was set for now. "Can you come over for dinner? I've been reading a few cookbooks, and I want to try making something. You've been feeding Tyler and me most nights, so it's our turn."

Carlos smiled. "Okay. That would be nice. Is there anything you want me to bring? I've got the stuff for a Caesar salad, and I make my own dressing for that as well, so I could bring that along if you like."

"Great." Billy Joe took the groceries into Carlos's apartment once he opened the door. Tyler followed, turned on the television, and climbed onto the sofa. The youngster seemed to have really made himself at home. Carlos thought it was because his television was bigger.

"Come on, Ty, we need to go home, but Mr. Carlos is going to come over for dinner," Billy Joe called.

Tyler climbed down off the sofa, looking completely put out. He half stomped over to them, fussing softly. Billy Joe picked him up indulgently and took him across the hall. Carlos closed the door and got to work making the salad he'd promised. Then he showered and dressed again, ready to knock on the door across the hall at the appointed time.

When Billy Joe opened it, Carlos went inside, accidentally brushing Billy Joe as he did. He paused and turned as Billy Joe touched his bare arm. He stayed still in case Billy Joe removed the heat that radiated through him from the simple touch. "Ummm...." He didn't want to scare Billy Joe off, but while Carlos was attracted to the cute southern boy with the wide green eyes and wavy light brown hair, he wasn't sure Billy Joe was ready for anything other than friendship.

"Where do you want this?" Carlos asked, holding still. It was nice being touched again. It had been a while, and he'd forgotten how something as simple as a touch on the arm could quicken his heartbeat and dry his mouth.

"I made room in the refrigerator," Billy Joe said without moving.

Carlos turned just enough to catch his intense gaze, creating a heated bubble that wound around both of them. "Okay."

He finally managed to move and took care of the dish and dressing. Tension and attraction had been building over the past few days. Carlos couldn't help noticing, but he hadn't acted on it, wondering if it was Billy Joe's inexperience or the fact that Carlos was the first gay man he'd met here, one who was open and didn't need to hide.

"What are you making? It smells good."

"It's a chicken dish with pineapple and stuff. I saw the recipe in the paper and thought it would be easy to make. I don't know if it's any good, but the smell is pretty hungrifying." Billy Joe got out some dishes and set them on the table.

"It does smell pretty amazing." Carlos's stomach rumbled loudly, and they both chuckled.

Billy Joe went to finish dinner, and Carlos wandered into the living room to see what Tyler was up to. He found Tyler playing on the floor with his cars and stuffed animals. Apparently the larger toys were obstacles in some sort of race course for the cars. Carlos sat on the sofa, letting Tyler play.

"When is his birthday?"

"Tyler will be three next month, December third," Billy Joe answered as he closed the oven door. "I think we have another fifteen minutes or so before it's done. At least according to the recipe." He came into the living room and sat next to Carlos, watching Tyler play as well. "I'm so lucky," he said quietly.

"I suppose you are. He's a wonderful little boy." Carlos glanced at Billy Joe, surprised at the set of his lips. His eyes were hard as flint, and Carlos wondered why.

"Yes. But he wouldn't have been… not if we'd have stayed." Billy Joe didn't look away from his son. "He would have been poisoned just like I was."

Carlos wasn't sure what Billy Joe was getting at. His hand shook and he turned slightly. That's when Carlos saw the slight bruising at his hairline near his ear. "What happened?" He couldn't help reaching out to touch it gently.

"My family," Billy Joe said quietly.

"They were here? They found you?" Carlos shifted closer. "What happened?" The questions came quickly as worry for Billy Joe and Tyler mounted every second Billy Joe remained quiet.

"No. They didn't find me... not like you think, but they're still here." Billy Joe placed his hand over his chest. "The bastards don't go away, and they won't just let me go." He seemed in honest discomfort, and Carlos struggled to figure out what could have caused it.

"You can talk to me," he offered, determined to let Billy Joe say what he wanted to.

Billy Joe nodded. "You know things are different here, especially near the university. Really different from back home." He sighed and shifted his gaze to the floor. "And... I took Tyler to the grocery store after I talked to you because I forgot some things and...." His cheeks pinked, and Carlos probably would have thought it adorable if Billy Joe wasn't in so much distress. "I had gotten my stuff and was checking out, and the woman behind the counter messed up and charged me twice for both of my items. I got angry and said... I wasn't nice. She was... black, and...." He groaned softly.

Carlos's eyes widened. "You didn't." He put his hand to his mouth.

"Yes. I apologized right away. I'd heard my dad saying things like that in my head all my life, and once I'd paid, I left the store in a hurry. I...." Billy Joe hung his head. "It just came out, and when I got back to the car, I was putting things in the trunk, paying more attention to what I'd said than what I was doing, and bashed my head on the trunk lid." He held his head between his hands. "I don't know what I was thinking. I got frustrated and it just came out." He clenched his fists. "I left home because I didn't want Tyler around that kind of stuff, and I did it myself as soon as someone made me angry."

Carlos wasn't sure what to say. It wasn't like he could tell Billy Joe that what he'd said was okay. It wasn't at all. But he also had to give Billy Joe credit for trying to overcome his upbringing. "Listen, it's—"

"It's not okay. This is why I left.... But what if I'm too stupid or had my head so filled with that stuff that I can't leave it behind?"

"I think you can."

"But I said—" Billy Joe swallowed.

Carlos wanted to step in and try to help, but he was only going to sound preachy and didn't want to do that. He figured Billy Joe's remorse and self-recrimination were enough for now. Billy Joe recognized he shouldn't have acted that way. As with many things in life, Carlos felt Billy Joe needed to come to terms with who he was and the kind of man he wanted to be.

"It will be all right." He took Billy Joe's hand, threading their fingers together. "It really will." He was pretty certain Billy Joe would find his way. "Come on. We should check on dinner." He held Billy Joe's hand as he stood and helped him up.

Billy Joe squeezed his fingers a little tighter and then let go, heading to the kitchen. He opened the oven and peered inside. "What do you think?"

Carlos checked it and grabbed a pot holder. He pulled the dish out and set it on the burners. "I think this looks awesome." It probably should have been served over rice, but Carlos didn't mention that. Billy Joe put hot pads in the center of the table and transferred the dish to there, while Carlos pulled his salad out of the refrigerator, dressed it, and put it on the table.

"Tyler, come for dinner," Billy Joe said rather quietly. When Tyler came running over, Billy Joe helped him into his seat. "I wanted this to be a celebration because I got a job." He dished out some chicken for Tyler and cut it up into small pieces, then set it aside to cool. Carlos put a few croutons from the salad in front of Tyler so he could eat them while he waited.

"No be sad, Daddy," Tyler said.

"I'll try."

Carlos took some of the chicken and salad for himself. "We all say stupid things sometimes. You apologized. The next time something happens to make you angry, remember this and you'll be fine." He placed a hand on top of Billy Joe's. "And you're not alone when it comes to overcoming some of the things our families drilled into our heads."

Carlos checked Tyler's plate and passed it to him, along with one of his spoons. Tyler started eating right away, making "nummy" sounds as he wolfed down the chicken and pineapple, leaving the peppers and bits of onion on his plate, which wasn't a surprise.

Billy Joe was quiet for a few minutes, and Carlos let him think. There was nothing uncomfortable about it, and Carlos helped Tyler with his dinner, giving him a few pieces of lettuce and gaping when Tyler ate it and asked for more. It seemed the kid liked his homemade dressing almost as much as Billy Joe did.

"Have they given you any indication of the kind of work you'll be doing?" Carlos asked, changing the subject to something brighter.

"Mr. Jackson said that I would be working with the electricians. He said that since I completed my course work and can prove it, I can get my apprenticeship completed and then I can apply for a license." The cloud that had settled over Billy Joe's face lifted and the sun came out in his eyes. "Once I get my license, I'll go up a pay grade. That will take a while, but he said he'd help make sure I get all the paperwork completed."

Carlos nodded. Marvin Jackson was a top-notch kind of guy in his opinion.

"He's a great guy. Lots of energy, and he's going to let me talk to some of the guys I'll be working with. Mr. Jackson seems like the kind of guy you want to do good work for." Billy Joe reached for the salad and took another helping. "Sounds a heck of a lot better than working for my dad. He's the kind of guy everyone on his teams tried to see how much they could get away with because they really don't care for him. Dad has trouble keeping real quality people 'cause he only wants to hire guys who think like him…."

Carlos chuckled. "And speak the same language." He understood exactly where Billy Joe was coming from. "I worked for some dipsticks in my time, and I left as soon as I could too." He took another helping of the chicken. "This is really good. You need to make this again."

"Is that what you do? Make things over and over?" Billy Joe asked.

"Sure. Learning to cook is about finding what works and what doesn't. I've made some real clinkers in my time, and I either figure out what's wrong or don't bother making them again." Carlos shrugged and took a bite. "It's only a meal, and if it doesn't turn out, it isn't the end of the world… well, most of the time. Unless you're cooking for someone important. Then even my mama would get frazzled in the kitchen."

He sighed, thinking about his mother. She was the only one he'd told he was leaving and why. Carlos had to give his mother credit that at least she'd tried to understand him, but only up to a point. She agreed that he had to go, but kept insisting that this was only a phase and that if he prayed to Saint This, Blessed That, he could be cured. In the end she'd turned her back on him, the same as the others.

Billy Joe gathered the dishes and then got a cloth to clean up Tyler. Carlos thought a hose might have been a more efficient solution, but that would be too cold. Once Tyler was wiped up, Billy Joe sent him to go play and finished clearing the table. They'd finished off the salad, and together they did the dishes and put everything away.

"Do you want to watch a movie? They hooked up the basic cable TV today. We can look at what's available." Billy Joe let the water out of the sink and rinsed it down. For some reason this unit didn't have a dishwasher—probably because the kitchen was so small. Carlos thought he should have offered to wash them at his place, but there were so few of them that this was easier anyway.

"Sounds awesome." Carlos wandered in to where Tyler was playing.

Billy Joe hung up the dishcloth and came into the living room. After finding the remote, he searched for a movie. "An action movie?"

"Explosions are always good. Are there any disaster movies on Netflix? Maybe *San Andreas*? They destroy Los Angeles and the Hoover Dam. All kinds of fictional mayhem and great special effects."

Billy Joe checked and turned, grinning. "It's here." He found the movie and queued it up. "I'm going to get Tyler ready for bed before we start." He took Tyler by the hand and led him into the bedroom. "I have Disney movies for Tyler until he gets sleepy."

Carlos wandered through the living room, looking at the few things Billy Joe had put out that were his own. Almost everything in the apartment was what came with it, but on the side table, Billy Joe had placed a baby picture of Tyler, and there was an old photograph of what Carlos suspected was Billy Joe riding a pony. It was an adorable picture. Billy Joe must have been six or seven. He lifted the frame to take a closer look and almost dropped it.

"Is there a Nazi flag in this picture?" Carlos asked, bringing it closer.

"Probably," Billy Joe said quietly from the doorway. "I remember riding that pony. It's one of my earliest happy memories, and Mom had my picture taken. She gave it to me when I had Tyler and said I needed to take him for a pony ride someday. Though I doubt I'll be taking Tyler to any white supremacist rallies at six or seven." He rolled his eyes. "What a shit family I have." He turned to Carlos. "Maybe we can scan the photo and crop it."

Carlos put the picture back, wiping his hands on his pants afterward. He felt a little dirty after handling it. He'd suspected that's what Billy Joe's family had been like, but to see proof of it, and from behind a picture of a child on a pony....

Billy Joe returned with Tyler in *Cars* pajamas that were a little too big for him. He climbed onto the sofa, and Billy Joe went to the shelf, lifted the photo, and placed it facedown in the drawer in the end table. Then he sat down on the other side of Tyler and started the Disney movie.

Tyler soon lost interest and slipped off the sofa to play on the floor. After half an hour, Tyler yawned, and Billy Joe paused the film and carried Tyler in to bed.

While he was waiting, Carlos went to the kitchen and grabbed fresh sodas and snacks, then turned off all the lights except the one in the corner.

Billy Joe came out a while later, closing the bedroom door most of the way, and started the action movie. "I'm sorry I kept you waiting, but—"

"It's all right."

Billy Joe took Carlos's hand, and Carlos forgot about the passage of time and how long he'd waited while Billy Joe put Tyler to bed. Nothing else seemed to matter except Billy Joe's work-roughened hands on his. The film continued, and Billy Joe shifted until they were leaning on each other.

About the time Los Angeles was left in ruins, an hour later, Billy Joe turned slightly, and Carlos moved to meet him. Their gazes met, and Carlos licked his lips. He leaned closer, and Billy Joe did the same until their lips touched.

Carlos started gentle, not wanting to scare Billy Joe off, but he was the one in for a slight shock as Billy Joe deepened the kiss, pressing him against the back cushions. Carlos wrapped Billy Joe in his arms, holding him tightly as the kiss deepened further. At this point Carlos couldn't have cared less what happened in the movie or anywhere else. The building could shake apart in an earthquake and he probably wouldn't have noticed.

Billy Joe tasted tangy on his tongue. Their kissing became more urgent by the second, and Carlos's control and discretion weakened the longer they were together. He tugged at Billy Joe's shirt, then slipped his hand underneath to caress his belly and chest.

"You feel so good," Carlos whispered, and Billy Joe pressed to him, pulling on Carlos's shirt as well.

A knocking from outside caught Carlos's attention, and he stopped. The sound came again, sounding like it was from across the hall, and Billy Joe groaned. Carlos sighed and straightened his clothes, then went to peer through the peephole.

He slowly opened the door. "What are you doing here?" Carlos asked as he stepped outside, leaving the door open slightly.

"I was told that this was your apartment," his cousin Luis said as he turned around, fixing Carlos with a hard look that left him wondering why in the hell he was here and what the fuck he wanted. "At least that's the address I was able to look up on the internet."

"I'm having dinner with a friend." Carlos felt Billy Joe behind him and turned to see him, with Tyler standing in the doorway, rubbing his eyes. "I'll be just a minute." He glared at his cousin, hoping Billy Joe and Tyler went back inside. "What do you want?" He crossed his arms over his chest.

Luis scowled. "Do we have to talk in the hallway?" He cocked his eyebrow, and Carlos ground his teeth at the way Luis held his nose in the air, as though coming here was beneath him.

"You aren't staying long," Carlos countered softly. "Tell me why you're here and what you want." He unlocked his apartment door and went inside, letting Luis follow. Luis had always thought of himself as the leader of their little group when they were kids. With the death of his father, Luis had taken over that side of the family. He thought he had the right to run everyone's life and was some sort of guardian of right and wrong… at least in the world according to Luis.

"Can I have something to drink? I know Aunt Teresa taught you better than this." Luis glared, but Carlos made no move.

"And I know Aunt Rosa didn't teach you to be a pompous ass. You came by that all on your own," Carlos said. "Now, tell me what you want and then get back on the broom you flew in on." He and Luis used to be friends, but that had ended long before Luis discovered Carlos was gay and decided to tell the rest of the family.

"Is that any way to talk to me?" Luis drew himself up to his full height. It was a classic intimidation technique, one that had worked on a younger Carlos, but now he just rolled his eyes.

"I don't want to talk to you at all." Carlos glanced at the door. He was going to give him a few more seconds and then tell Luis to leave, but knowing his cousin, he'd just come back again and again. It was best to get him to spit out what he came to say.

Luis leaned forward. "You think I wanted to come here? I'd rather eat dirt. But you never answer your phone, and this was the only address we could find. Six years and you tell no one anything. Just a card for Juan's fifteenth birthday and that's it."

"Juan's a good kid. Always has been," Carlos said. His youngest brother had been amazing growing up. Carlos had no idea what he was like now. He shook away the memories that threatened to wash back like a flood. He'd put those aside for a reason, and they needed to stay there. His family had abandoned him, and regardless of what Luis said or how he might try to twist things, that was what happened. "Luis… why are you here? If seeing me is so distasteful, why did you come? I don't need you or any of the rest of the family."

Luis sighed with a soft huff. Whatever the reason, it was damn near killing Luis to have to come see him. Carlos liked that idea just a little bit.

"Carlos, are you all right?" Billy Joe asked from across the hall.

"Yes." Carlos motioned, and Billy Joe stepped over. "This is my oldest cousin, Luis." Carlos did his best to look uninterested. "Luis, this is—" He stumbled a second as to how to introduce him.

"I'm Carlos's boyfriend," Billy Joe interjected. "And you're interrupting… things." Billy Joe stepped in front of Luis to stand next to him.

Carlos hadn't been expecting that… neither the backup nor the boyfriend thing. He and Billy Joe hadn't talked about things like that at all. He wondered for a second if that was strictly for Luis's benefit.

Luis paled beautifully, his normally dark complexion turning waxy. His lip curled upward, baring his teeth.

"Please, are you a dog, growling?" Billy Joe asked. "My dipshit family does that all the time when they're angry."

Carlos did his best to keep from snorting and failed, which only made Luis huffier. "Enough pleasantries…." Carlos turned to Luis. "Why did you come all this way?"

"I didn't. I was in Philadelphia on some business and—"

"You thought you'd pay me a visit." Carlos rolled his eyes. "Just spit it out."

Luis ground his teeth. God, this game was getting fun. Maybe if Carlos continued to pick on him, Luis's head would explode. The vein on his forehead was already throbbing, and the muscles protruded on his neck. Carlos waited, stepping closer to Billy Joe. He needed to let Luis say his piece so he could get rid of him.

"I told everyone this was stupid and that you wouldn't help us."

"I don't even know what you want," Carlos said softly.

"Why would he help you with anything?" Billy Joe asked. "You ran him out of town because you didn't want a gay cousin around." He stared daggers at Luis. "Yes, he told me what happened."

"Did he tell you he ran out in the middle of the night?" Luis countered. "He left like some thief…."

"Bullshit, Luis. I talked to my mom—she knew I was leaving. The only person I ran out on was you and your closet." Carlos had had enough, and Luis blanching hard was a huge reward. "Say what you came here to say. You seem to think you need my help." He just wanted Luis to go and get the hell out of his life.

Luis ignored his remark, opened his coat, and pulled out some papers, folded lengthwise. He opened them and passed them to Carlos. "The family has decided to sell some of our land outside of town to a developer. It was the original farm that our grandparents bought. The land was left to everyone, and because your father passed away, we need you to sign off." He pulled out a pen. "Just sign it so the rest of us can get on with things."

Carlos didn't take the pen. "What is this?"

"You're no longer a part of the family. This is a paper that states that you relinquish all claims to the property." Luis pressed the pen forward, hovering over him. "Just sign it!" he repeated, this time with more menace.

It was so tempting to sign the paper just to get Luis to go and to have his family out of his hair forever. Carlos had no doubt that if he didn't, he'd end up with God knew how many complications out of this. Whatever the land was, it was something he hadn't even known about.

"My mother and your mother need the money this deal is going to bring in so they can stop working and have a chance at a retirement. But by following the various wills, you have a part interest in the land. We need you to give up your portion," Luis said, sounding so reasonable.

"Bullshit," Billy Joe said. "You come in here and expect him to sign over whatever this is to you just because you want it?" He placed his hand on Carlos's shoulder. "This sounds fishier than the opening day of catfish season."

Carlos glared at the papers. "Write the address on the back, and if I decide to sign, I'll send the papers." God, it felt good to have a little backup. "I need to have this looked over."

"It's for your mother," Luis said.

"No. You never did a damn thing for anyone that didn't involve you getting some piece of it for yourself." Carlos felt his backbone returning. "I have friends who can look into this, and once I know what's going on, I'll make my decision. But—" He stepped closer and waited while Luis wrote an address on the back of the papers. "—you show up here again and the answer is no. You got that? I don't want to see your closet-case ass anywhere near me again."

Luis smacked him across the cheek. "You cut that gay shit out. I have a wife and two kids. You're the perverted one."

Carlos rubbed his cheek and smiled. When Luis relaxed, he brought his knee right into Luis's groin, sending him to the floor. "Go home to your wife and explain to her why you aren't going to be having a third. But tell her the whole truth. Or maybe I'll send a note with the papers explaining just the kind of man you were in high school. Maybe your wife will rip your tiny, pea-sized little nuts off. Remember, I know some of your secrets." He stepped back to let Luis get up, but he just groaned. "You have your answer. Now get the hell out." Carlos wasn't going to stay in the same room with Luis any longer.

"Sign the papers and send them back. Otherwise...." Luis slowly stood, his legs shaking.

"Otherwise nothing. You have no power here, and I'm not intimidated by you any longer. I have my own life here, a career, and friends. You and the rest of the family rejected me. Remember that."

Luis snatched forward, but Carlos jumped back. "So help me, I'll—"

"You'll nothing. Every one of you turned your back because I was gay. You didn't want a *maricón* in your family. Well, now you don't have one. I stopped being your cousin when you threw me away. My own mother did the same thing, and so did yours. And they want my help, but right now I'm not inclined to give it."

Carlos stepped closer. "Leave. You'll get my decision in the mail. And no matter what it is, don't come back here." He walked to the door and held it open.

Luis left, and Carlos watched him descend the stairs, then heard the front door of the building opening and closing. He waited to see if his cousin would return, but the stairs remained empty. Carlos leaned on the doorframe, sighing softly.

"You really handled him," Billy Joe said quietly from behind him.

"No. I got angry and let that take over." Carlos wiped his eyes. "Luis was an ass to push me out of the family. But I shouldn't have hit him. I really burned that bridge, didn't I?" He shook his head. "I should...."

Billy Joe took his hand and led him across the hall into his apartment. He guided Carlos to the old sofa, sat him down, and hurried away. When he came back inside, he sat next to him. "I closed your apartment door."

"I think I should be alone."

"No, I don't think so," Billy Joe argued.

"I don't know what I'm going to do." Carlos groaned, holding his head in his hands. It occurred to him that after all this time, he'd still hoped his family would take him back. "I can never go back now." The doors were completely closed to him. Luis was going to see to that. "What shocks me is that I thought I was over them. That I had moved on. And yet Luis shows up, asshole that he is, and part of me was hoping he would ask me to come home. That my family realized they were wrong and wanted me to be part of their lives again." He stood to pace the small room. "All they wanted was to make kicking me out official." He clenched his hands into fists, shaking them as he tried to work through what all this meant.

"Did you really think your family might change their minds? I know mine never will." Billy Joe sat close to him. "People don't change their mind over what they think are the big, important things."

58

Carlos scratched his head. "What I don't get is why people think that what someone else does behind closed doors is so important to them. It's no one else's business, and yet my family and everyone they know seem to think it's their right to tell me who I love." He dropped his hand, clenching a fist once again, groaning in frustration. "I thought my mother would come to understand that I was still her son and that she should love me for me."

"Mine will go along with whatever my dad says."

"My dad passed away, and my mother is so stubborn." Carlos paced some more. "She likes to be in charge of everything and everyone. I swear she tried to pick out Luis's wife for him. Deciding who was good enough and who didn't measure up for my cousin—along with his mother, of course. He married who he did simply because she was the first girl both women approved of. Who cared what he thought? Not that it really matters, because Luis isn't going to be happy with a woman. He'll delude himself and all that shit, but end up miserable."

"He really likes guys?" Billy Joe asked.

Carlos snickered. "The man can suck dick like a vacuum cleaner." He pursed his lips, and Billy Joe smiled and then started chuckling. "That's usually a dead giveaway. Guys who hide part of themselves like that usually aren't going to be happy. But I honestly wish Luis and his family the best in Amarillo, especially if they stay there." He had no real interest in a repeat performance. Carlos turned toward a still-chuckling Billy Joe. "I appreciate you coming over. It made standing up to him a lot easier." Though he had actually been tempted to sign just to get Luis to go away and never come back, that probably wasn't the best thing to do. Billy Joe had given him strength.

Billy Joe shrugged. "It was the right thing."

Carlos nodded, going over the encounter in his head. "Did you mean what you said to Luis, or was that just something to try to wind him up? About being my boyfriend, I mean." Carlos would understand if that was something off the cuff that Billy Joe thought would get under Luis's skin, because it really had. Carlos had thought Luis would choke on his tongue.

"I meant it. I probably should have asked you first…." Billy Joe bit his lower lip. "It just came out. I guess I should have talked to you about it before I just blurted it out to your cousin—"

Carlos leaned closer and kissed Billy Joe quiet. "It was nice. I liked it." He smiled and kissed Billy Joe once again, exploring his lips and tasting his richness. "I haven't had much luck with relationships."

Billy Joe sighed, his heated breath warming Carlos's lips. "I never had one, not really. I was with Tyler's mother, but she wasn't really a girlfriend even." He closed his eyes. "I feel bad for what I did to her. Not that I hurt her or anything… at least not physically. But I know that I ended up hurting her in the end." Billy Joe tugged him closer, hugging Carlos tightly. "I've done a really good job of messing up things in my life so far. But I've done my best to try not to hurt people."

"Considering how you grew up…." Carlos's gaze shifted to the side table, where the picture had been. "I'd say that was a sort of miracle." He knew what those groups were capable of.

"At least I did right by Tyler." Billy Joe sighed.

Carlos backed away slightly. "Did you ever have… well, someone you were close to? A friend, maybe a special friend?"

Billy Joe nodded.

"Do you think he would keep your secret if you called him? Maybe having someone from back home who you could trust would help you. I mean, I can try…." Carlos was messing this up. "I'm just saying that sometimes having a touchstone, someone you aren't interested in… as a boyfriend… is a good thing. It gives you perspective."

Billy Joe shook his head. "I did have someone like that, but I can't call them." He tugged Carlos close once again, their heat mixing. Carlos's heart beat faster as he inhaled Billy Joe's earthy male scent. His cock hardened, and he shifted his hips so he wasn't pressing his dick against Billy Joe, not sure if he was ready for that. Judging by the hardness he encountered, it wasn't an issue. Damn, Billy Joe was a big boy.

"Okay." Carlos captured Billy Joe's lips in a kiss that sent him reeling. Billy Joe might not have had much experience, but he sure knew how to kiss. Carlos quivered at the energy in it, the pressure, the way Billy Joe moved his lips just enough to drive Carlos crazy. He moaned softly, trying not to make noise and yet unable to keep completely quiet. Carlos pulled away, breathing heavily, his mind clouding with desire. "I think I better go," he whispered.

Billy Joe's mouth hung open, and he lowered his gaze. "I'm sorry. If I was too rough or...."

Carlos smiled, taking another deep breath to calm the storm that swirled inside. He needed some distance, and quickly. "It's not that." He lowered his voice. "If I don't leave, I'm going to go too far, and I don't think you want Tyler waking up to find you bareassed with me on top of you, and...." Even saying the words threatened to push his control over the edge. He swallowed. "Like I said, I think it's best if I go home now." Carlos stood, adjusting his pants. Billy Joe couldn't help but see the extent of his arousal.

"Oh." Billy Joe shifted a little and then stood. Holy cow. His pants were indecent, and Carlos turned away, heading toward the door. "I'll see you tomorrow?" Billy Joe asked.

Carlos nodded, his hands shaking. "I'll get my dishes then." He left the apartment, headed right to his, and closed and locked the door behind him. "Jesus." He hadn't expected that. Billy Joe had kissed him—well, they'd kissed each other, but.... He leaned against the door, calming the hormone rush as best he could and at the same time berating himself for leaving in the first place.

"It was the right thing to do," he told himself out loud. There was no need to rush, and Billy Joe deserved more than some quick grope on the sofa. Carlos took a deep breath, blew it out, and closed his eyes. Then he pushed away from the door and went to the bathroom to splash a little water on his face before brushing his teeth and getting ready for bed. He intended to crawl into bed, but stripped down and started the shower instead.

The water felt amazing, and Carlos washed his hair, then stepped under the water, rinsing away the shampoo, letting the spray cascade down on him as he wondered what Billy Joe was doing now. God, he needed to get his head on straight, but damn, it was hard to think clearly with Billy Joe just across the hall. Carlos had been seconds from pushing him down on the cushions and kissing the life out of him while he tugged at Billy Joe's clothes. Carlos wanted to maul him, to see what he hid under those worn jeans and ill-fitting shirt.

Carlos let his hands wander down his chest. He wrapped his fingers around his cock as his imagination went to work. He closed his eyes, and soon his own hands were Billy Joe's, touching him, squeezing his length just right, pressing against him. Carlos's legs shook as he gave his mind free rein. His skin tingled from the water and from everywhere his hands roamed. Carlos lowered his head, lips pulling back to take in as much air as he could, pent-up desire and want building inside him.

He ran his grip over his length, wishing Billy Joe were kissing him, pressing to his back. He imagined that thick cock he'd felt earlier gliding into him, sliding up and down. Pressure was already building, and he wanted it to last. This was too delicious a fantasy to let go of. He needed to hold on to it for as long as he could. Not that he didn't fantasize, but this was the first time in a while that his thoughts wrapped around him and were so alive and nearly real that they made his legs shake and his breath hitch. Pure and simple, he wanted Billy Joe in the worst way—touching him, holding him, talking to him… all of it. The more he thought about it, the more excited he got, until he could no longer hold off, coming unglued and crying out in his release until it echoed off the walls.

Carlos blinked, breathing like he'd run a marathon. He leaned against the tile, water still sluicing over him. Eventually he could think again, and finished cleaning up, turned off the water, and wrapped a towel around his waist. Man, if that was what his imagination conjured up, what was the real thing going to be like? Carlos dried off and pulled on a pair of light sweats and an old T-shirt, then padded out to get a snack before settling on the sofa. He ended up lying down to watch television and fell asleep right there, too tired to go in to bed.

CHAPTER 5

BILLY JOE stared down at his new driver's license. Now that he had that, he needed to go get new plates. But dang, that was a pain in the rear. Apparently, DMV services here in Pennsylvania were completely hosed up. One couldn't actually get license plates and driver's licenses in the same place. What a pain.

"How was work?" Carlos asked as he climbed the stairs.

"Busy. There's a huge backlog of work to be done, and so much of it needs to be completed before winter." Billy Joe turned to peer inside to where Tyler was coloring at the table. "Which is awesome." He turned back to Carlos. "They have me working overtime next week while the kids are out on break to try to handle the backlog, but the day care closes at six, and...."

"It's okay. Add me as someone who can pick up Tyler, and I'll get him before they close and just bring him to my place. He can stay with me until you get home. It will be fine. I have a few things to do, but it's largely a holiday for me, so we can work out a schedule. Maybe have him there half days?"

"I think I can do that," Billy Joe said.

"Do you have to work Thanksgiving?"

"No." Billy Joe was grateful for that at least. "Do you have plans?"

"Sort of. I usually have some friends over from work. They don't really have the time to go back home to see families on the other side of the country, so they come over here. Angie from the library and her husband, Andy. Their families are in California. And Marie, who heads the circulation desk. You and Tyler should join us. Andy watches football, and the rest of us sit around and gab."

Billy Joe sighed. "That would be great." He'd been worried that Carlos would have big plans somewhere and he'd end up sitting at home for his first big holiday away from his family, with nothing to do. "What do I bring?"

Carlos chuckled. "I was hoping that you and Tyler would help. Maybe let me use your oven if I need it." He smiled. "Maybe if Andy wants to watch football, he could do that at your place and then we could let Tyler watch stuff here." He sounded so excited. Carlos obviously loved to entertain.

"Of course—that's fine." Billy Joe shifted his weight from foot to foot. They still had dinner together most nights, unless Carlos had evening hours, and then Billy Joe would make him a sandwich for when he got home just so he knew Carlos got something to eat. The guy worked really hard, and the students came before food.

"I got the stuff for a pot roast for tomorrow. I'm going to put it in the Crock-Pot and let it cook. But I'm stymied as to what to have for dinner tonight." Carlos leaned on his doorframe, looking really drawn and tired. "My mother called me today, asking about those papers." He groaned. "I wish they would leave me alone."

Billy Joe did too. This wasn't the first time they had tried contacting Carlos, with different family members working on him each time. "Tell them you'll never sign that paper, and you'll only sign off on the actual sale of the property as long as you get your share in cash. Make them pay you. If they want to sell, then you deserve your rightful inheritance. It came from your grandpa."

"I've thought the same thing. Angie said I should get a lawyer down there and let him handle it. At least he could look into the details of the deed and what the land is worth. Make sure I'm covered. But that's just complicating the situation." Carlos sighed again. "I said they had better leave me alone until after the holidays or I was never going to sell and they could all rot as far as I was concerned." He smiled finally, sending a little thrill through Billy Joe. "Why don't we order pizza for tonight? I've had enough thinking about family and stuff. We're both off tomorrow, so I thought we could get in the car and take Tyler up to Hershey. Let him go to Chocolate World to ride the ride and see the shows. He can get some chocolate and look at the streetlights shaped like Kisses."

"That would be awesome." Billy Joe sighed slightly. "I just have to find a place that will help me register my car. I'm working so much that it's difficult."

Carlos nodded. "It's a pain here. Let me call the dealership I bought my last car from. They might be able to handle it for you. They do that sort of thing all the time, and they're open on Saturday." Carlos unlocked his door and pushed it open.

"Then I'll call for the pizza, and we'll meet as soon as it comes." That sounded like a plan to Billy Joe, and from the weary nod he got from Carlos, he was grateful as well.

"I'll see you then." Carlos leaned over to give him a quick kiss and a wink before going in his apartment. Billy Joe's heart skipped a little as he went inside as well.

"What do you think of pizza with Mr. Carlos for dinner?" he asked Tyler, who looked up from where he was coloring as intently as if he were painting the Mona Lisa.

"Yes." Tyler titled his head slightly, like he was puzzled. "You kissed Mr. Carlos." He giggled. "That's yucky. I don't want to kiss anybody... not on the lips. It's slimy." He went back to his coloring after that little pronouncement.

"Kissing is not slimy. Do your lips feel slimy?" Billy Joe smiled. Tyler seemed to be lost in his own coloring world once again, so Billy Joe let him be. He looked up the number of the pizza place that Carlos liked and placed an order, then set about making a small salad to bring over. He sat with Tyler, watching him work, until his phone buzzed with a message that the pizzas were there. "Gather your things." He took Tyler by the hand and went with him to get the pizza. They returned to Carlos's, knocked, and went inside. He set the pizzas on the table. "Dinner is here."

"Be right out."

Tyler raced to the television, turned it on, and plopped down in front of it, intently watching, as Billy Joe got the salad and locked his door. When he returned, Carlos was on the phone, looking even more frazzled than he had been before.

"You know, you won't leave me alone, so here's the deal. I will sign nothing except a document agreeing to the sale of my portion. That's right. You want me to sign off, so buy me out, and I mean at full market value. I'm through dealing with any of you, Luis. That's what I want. Otherwise you can all go to hell." Carlos pulled the phone away from his ear. "Great, if it's worth two million and I own 15 percent, then send me three hundred grand, not a penny less. And my price will go up by twenty grand for every phone call I receive from anyone about this. Do you understand? You threaten me, it costs twenty grand. Beg, cajole, be a pain in the ass... pay me. I'm done with all of you selfish bastards." He sighed and pulled the phone away from his ear once again. Billy Joe could hear the yelling from across the room. "Take it or leave it. That's my last word on the subject. I'll get a lawyer, and you can deal with him if you want to go that route." He jabbed the screen of his phone and tossed it onto the sofa, shaking. "They just won't back off." Billy Joe hugged him, wishing he could make this better, but there was little he could do except support him the way Carlos had been helping him.

Billy Joe got out plates and glasses and opened the pizza boxes. "Come on, Tyler. Turn off the television for dinner." He waited for Carlos to sit as he got Tyler settled as well. "You know you can just not take their calls," Billy Joe said. "If you don't want to talk to them, then don't." He had no intention of taking any phone calls from his family.

"I know. I think it's residual guilt, but maybe they'll leave me alone for a while before they launch their next assault." Carlos grinned and took a bite of his pizza.

THEY'D MIGRATED to Billy Joe's place to put Tyler to bed. He'd been read a number of stories from both Billy Joe and Carlos. Tyler had figured out that Carlos had a soft spot for story time. Must be the librarian in him.

They sat on the sofa, the television on low. Billy Joe half watched the new episode of *Will and Grace*. Carlos laughed as Grace and Karen ended up locked together in the shower. Billy Joe barely noticed their antics, wondering what it would be like to be locked in a shower with Carlos. For one thing, there would be a lot less clothing, at least in his imagination.

The episode ended, and Carlos turned to him, heat radiating from his body. Billy Joe's own body reacted to the heat and spicy scent that curled around his senses, drawing him closer.

Carlos closed the distance between them and wrapped his arms around him. "I want you," Carlos whispered.

Billy Joe nodded. He knew that. He wanted Carlos too, but Tyler was in his own bed, in the single bedroom they shared. Billy Joe sighed. The heat built instantly before Carlos's lips touched his. Anticipation was delicious, and they had driven it to new heights. When Carlos kissed him, Billy Joe's capacity to think and breathe flew out the window, though he didn't mind in the least. He pressed Carlos against the sofa cushions, his ability to hold back from Carlos waning quickly. He tugged at Carlos's shirt, desperately needing skin-on-skin contact. "We can't do this here."

"Huh…?" Carlos breathed.

"Tyler has been getting up the last few days." Billy Joe wasn't ashamed of being with Carlos. Tyler had seen them kiss, but he didn't want to have to explain why his hand was down Carlos's pants.

Carlos climbed off the sofa, muted the television, then tugged Billy Joe to his feet and guided him into the bathroom. Carlos closed the door and pressed Billy Joe against the back of it. Billy Joe blinked and gasped as Carlos kissed him hard. It was only the bathroom, but they were finally alone, behind a locked door. Tyler was in the next room, but....

Dammit, he was thinking of Tyler as Carlos tugged his shirt off.

Carlos turned on the water in the shower, then pulled off his own shirt and kicked off his shoes. Billy Joe humphed as Carlos barreled into him, clutching him to his heated body.

Billy Joe closed his eyes, letting the sensation of Carlos carry him away. Sometimes being a father, with all its worries, got overwhelming, and Carlos's hands on him, the tingles left behind by each touch, carried those worries away for now. Billy Joe's legs shook as Carlos reached for his belt, tugged it open, and then unfastened his pants. He'd lost a little weight since coming here because his jeans slid right down his legs, pooling on the floor. He stepped out of them, rocking back and forth as he tried to get his feet untangled from the damn things.

Carlos took that moment to check the water temperature, then stood in front of him. "I'm nervous," he whispered shakily.

So was Billy Joe, but he stripped off the last of his clothes, standing naked in front of Carlos. For a second he tried to remember the last time he was this completely bare in front of anyone. Billy Joe had been hiding behind his clothes, his attitude, and his bravado for years and years. He knew the truth, and now he'd stripped away the last of his armor, standing naked in front of Carlos, hoping he liked what he saw.

Carlos stepped back, stripped off his pants, and stepped into the shower, holding the curtain aside for him. Billy Joe stepped under the water as well. At first he'd wondered if Carlos was shy, but he tugged Billy Joe into a hug, holding him, running his hands slowly up and down his back.

"I've wondered what it would be like to do this for weeks," Carlos whispered, letting his head fall back under the water, stretching his lean, toned body, pressing his hips to Billy Joe's.

"Me too." Billy Joe stepped back, reached for the soap, and lathered his hands. Then he placed them on Carlos's chest, soaping him up. "I used to hide these magazines that I got at a bookstore. I only had two of them, and I hid them away from the house. There was an old cabin a little ways from home, and I used to go there. That way, if they were found, no one would know whose they were. I hid them well." He closed his eyes again, letting his hands continue to roam, taking in each contour.

But when Carlos gasped, Billy Joe had to watch. His eyes snapped open as he ran his fingers over Carlos's nipples, his moan mingling with the sound of the water.

"Billy Joe, that's so good."

"There were pictures of two men in the shower," Billy Joe said, turning Carlos around, pressing to his back while he slid his hands up and down his chest. "They stood like this, and I used to imagine what it would be like to have someone of my own to hold that way." He pushed closer, his fingers brushing the wet curls at the base of Carlos's cock. "I was so alone and I wanted someone to hold, someone who would be mine." He bent his head forward to kiss Carlos's honey-brown shoulder.

"Is this what you imagined?" Carlos asked, his voice quivering.

"More." Billy Joe swallowed hard, then kissed him again. He didn't let his fingers wander over Carlos's cock—that was an experience he wanted to savor. Instead, he slid them upward to pluck Carlos's nipples, sending amazing waves of pleasure that rippled through both of them. "It's so much more." He squeezed Carlos even tighter and then loosened his hold, not wanting to hurt him.

Carlos turned slowly in his arms. "I used to dream of something like this too." He slid his hands along Billy Joe's cheeks, then cupped his head gently before bringing their lips together in a searing kiss that only added more heat and steam to the shower. Carlos slowly moved him back, and Billy Joe went willingly, the rising warmth in Carlos's eyes burning through Billy Joe.

The tile was still cool on his back, but it did little to dampen the desire that raced through him. He groaned softly, and Carlos must have assumed it was desire. Billy Joe kissed him even harder, inhaling deeply, letting everything about Carlos surround his senses, including the way his cock slid along Carlos's. That was glorious and so very different from the feel of his own hand.

"God...," Billy Joe groaned, thrusting his hips forward for a little more sensation. Carlos met his movements, shifting up and down in a breath-stealing dance. Billy Joe, fearing he'd fall, stopped moving, leaning against the tile. Carlos chuckled and backed away.

Billy Joe was afraid he was going to leave out of frustration or something, but Carlos only reached for the soap. He lathered his hands and ran them over Billy Joe's chest. Billy Joe braced himself against the wall, using it to hold himself up. He needed the stability when his knees wobbled. Carlos's hands roamed downward, and he stilled, holding his breath as Carlos wound his fingers around his length and stroked him slowly.

"Oh my God," Billy Joe whimpered.

"Damn, you're...." Carlos groaned as Billy Joe clamped his eyes closed, desperately trying to keep from embarrassing himself. Carlos had barely touched him and he was already seconds from coming.

"Please stop or I'm going to come...," Billy Joe pleaded.

Carlos stopped moving, still gripping Billy Joe's cock. "I want you to come. I want to see you fly over the edge. I bet you look amazing," he whispered and moved his hand once again, this time with more force.

Dang, there was no way Billy Joe was going to be able to resist. His legs shook as his release got closer and closer, pressure building until he couldn't control it any longer. "Oh God!" He whimpered between gritted teeth as he came as hard as he could ever remember.

His head swam, and the passion only increased when Carlos guided him under the water. The heat and wet mixed with his tingling skin to nearly drive him out of his mind. Billy Joe hissed until the sensation passed. "What about you?" Carlos's arousal was plain, pressing to his hip. Billy Joe slid his hand between them, wrapped his fingers around the thick cock, and let the smooth hardness slide along his fingers.

"Man…," Carlos groaned in his ear. "That's so good." They held each other to stay upright.

Billy Joe paused and slowly sank to his knees to take Carlos between his lips.

"You don't…." The words trailed off in a long, soft moan as Billy Joe slid his lips down the thick length. He had little experience and went slow. That didn't seem to matter to Carlos, judging by the way he trembled. Damn, that was exciting in itself, and Billy Joe felt his cock returning to life. But this wasn't about him right now—this was about Carlos, and damned if the man didn't throw himself into his pleasure just like he seemed to with everything else.

Carlos rocked back and forth enough that Billy Joe grabbed his firm buttcheeks to help to set the pace. It was amazing how easily they understood each other. Even the pacing of sex seemed almost intuitive.

"Billy Joe…," Carlos gasped.

Billy Joe found he loved the feeling of Carlos's cock sliding along his tongue. He closed his eyes and gave himself over to the experience of bringing Carlos pleasure. He seemed to fill the shower with soft sighs and groans, which only heightened Billy Joe's own pleasure and excitement. He kept up the pace, taking him as deeply as he dared, thrilled at the guttural moan he received when he nearly got all of Carlos's length at one time.

"Not long...," Carlos warned, and Billy Joe backed off, stroked him as he stood, and brought their lips together in a take-no-prisoners kiss. Carlos quivered through his release, nearly biting Billy Joe's lips in his intensity.

When he stilled, Billy Joe gently guided him under the spray. They were both clean by this point, so he turned off the water and stepped out of the shower. He retrieved two towels from under the sink and wrapped Carlos in the largest one, and then dried himself.

Billy Joe gathered their clothes, handing Carlos his. "I didn't expect our first time to be in the shower."

Carlos chuckled. "Me neither, but if I'd had to keep my hands off you for about two seconds longer, I think I was going to explode. Do you have any idea how hard it's been to sit next to you and smell that cologne you wear all the damn time and not say 'to hell with it' and jump you?"

"I don't wear cologne," Billy Joe said with a slight smile, loving how Carlos's eyes darkened even further.

"Damn...." Carlos pulled on his underwear. "That's all you." He closed his eyes and then hugged Billy Joe tight. "I could smell you all the damn time. It turns me on." He tightened his grip, cupping Billy Joe's butt and squeezing slightly.

"Shhh." Billy Joe stilled, listening intently, thinking he might have heard Tyler. He stepped back, pulled on the rest of his clothes, and cracked the door to listen.

"Daddy?"

The call was faint, and Billy Joe went right into the bedroom where Tyler sat up in bed, the cover pulled up to his chin, eyes wide.

"A man was outside."

"Sweetheart, we're on the second floor. That was probably just the shadows from the trees." He pointed as the leaves and branches moved against the shade. He hugged Tyler and settled him back down into bed. "That's all. Just the tree and leaves. Nothing more."

He soothed Tyler back to sleep, and once he rolled over, Billy Joe left the room, leaving the door cracked open.

"Is he okay?" Carlos asked.

"Yeah. Most of the leaves have fallen, so the branches and things cast shadows into the room, and they're scarier now. He's taken to waking up a few times in the night, and lately he's asked for Gran." Billy Joe sat on the sofa. "I'm never sure what to tell him. He loves his gran and grampy. I know he does, even if my dad gets gruff sometimes, but…." Billy Joe was at a complete loss.

"They show him what they want him to see. You know them for who they really are." Carlos straightened his shirt and sat next to him. "I have to ask…."

Billy Joe followed Carlos's gaze to the drawer. It was like that damn picture had some sort of magnetic power even if it was out of sight.

"I can guess what sort of upbringing you had, and those beliefs have to be very ingrained."

Billy Joe nodded. "They are, I guess. I heard the gospel according to white power my entire life. I can tell you where everyone who's different belongs." He made a face that looked like he'd eaten something bad, like dirt. "Blacks should be kept in their place. People like you should be sent back where they came from…. Jews…." Billy Joe's voice faltered. "My dad said the Nazis should be allowed to finish the job." He shook his head. "I used to believe that shit. I did. I thought they were right. I was a kid and had it poured into me. I heard it my entire life. But it's wrong. I know that. My dad and the people I thought were part of my family… are wrong!"

"I get that…." Carlos nodded and leaned closer. "But how did you figure that out? I mean, I know it's wrong too, but you don't give up years of indoctrination overnight." Carlos took his hand. "I'm just trying to understand part of who you are. That kind of self-examination is pretty rare."

He was self-aware? Billy Joe stifled a scoff. More like he'd had the piss, shit, snot, and anything else unpleasant scared the fuck out of him. "I…. Well, I mean, I really don't fit in with my family because I'm gay…." He sighed. "You have no idea how long it was before I could even allow myself to admit that in my own head. I used to pray that God would fix me." He felt himself paling and then sniffed as he tried to hold back a huge wave of grief that seemed to be getting larger every second he tried to keep it at bay.

"I think a lot of us go through that." Carlos put his arm around him, tugging him until Billy Joe leaned on him. "No one wants to be different."

"That's what Hilliard said." Just saying the name out loud sent cracks in the dike of his emotions. Billy Joe stiffened and remembered he was supposed to be strong. He didn't want to bring all this shit with his family everywhere he went. "He was a friend of mine. The first person I knew who was gay, and he was out and proud, even in Jackson. Hilliard went to Ole Miss— University of Mississippi—and he saw me at a coffee shop. I looked at him for what must have been too long, and I saw him looking back, hard."

"Did the two of you ever… get together?" Carlos asked, tugging a little tighter. Billy Joe thought Carlos might be jealous or something.

"No. Things weren't like that with him and me. We had coffee sometimes and talked. He was dating someone else. The thing was, I had to keep that friendship a secret from my dad, so Hilliard never came to the house or anything. But Hilliard, more than anyone, helped me realize some of who I was. He was so patient." Billy Joe smiled.

"There's a story there," Carlos said. "I mean, it's a wonder you even got to be friends at all."

Billy Joe sniffed again. "He saved my life. Pulled me from in front of an oncoming car."

That day had been the very worst of his life, the lowest of the low, the bottom of the barrel. He buried his face in Carlos's shoulder. Damn it all. He wasn't going to cry over things he couldn't help or change. Getting out and making a better life for Tyler was in large part due to Hilliard, and he wasn't going to dishonor his memory and strength by whimpering like a baby. Hilliard deserved so much more than that.

"That must have been terrifying," Carlos told him softly.

Billy Joe nodded. He'd gotten out and was going to make the most of it. Let Carlos think that was why he was so damned upset. He wasn't going to unload the massive pile of shit that was his life back in Mississippi. Billy Joe had done his best to leave all that in the past, and that was where it needed to stay—forever, if possible.

"It was." He pulled away, wiping his eyes. "Afterward, he helped me get my feet under me, and we ended up in the same coffee shop where I first saw him. It was near Ole Miss, with a lot of students in it. I didn't want to go at first. I knew in my gut that he was gay like me, and that scared the shit out of me. But he was nice, and I needed a chance to deal with what had happened. Hilliard bought me a coffee, sat with me in the corner, and listened. Sometimes it's easier to tell shit to a stranger you think you're never going to see again."

"Was this before you had Tyler?" Carlos asked.

"It was while Carol Ann was pregnant and I didn't know what I was going to do. Everyone told me to marry her, but I couldn't. I knew there was something wrong with me and…." Some of the darkness that had engulfed his soul that day washed back over him, settling on his shoulders like a lead weight, pressing his spirit down deep inside until it threatened to touch his soul the way it had that day. He couldn't allow that. Billy Joe resolutely pulled himself back, pushing the despair where it belonged—in the past. "Hilliard understood and listened. He told me that no matter what, I had to lead my own life. I used to meet him once a week there after work and we'd talk. It was nice having a friend, and he was the first person I told I was gay. Hilliard told me he was proud of me for opening up and helped me accept what I could about the situation."

"Did he know about your family?" Carlos asked.

Billy Joe shook his head. "He knew how they felt, and that was enough. I was never going to introduce them. It would only make things worse for me, and bad for Hilliard." Billy Joe cleared his throat, pushing that darkness away once again. The past was the past. "He was a good friend." He dried his eyes. "So you see, the person I am, and this self-aware guy you seem to think I am, is because of him. Hilliard never made me feel badly for wanting to love my family or for believing them. He never said anything untrue. Hilliard was there for me, someone who listened. He helped me untie the knot inside of me." Billy Joe seemed worn out and yawned, followed quickly by another.

"I should let you get some rest." Carlos leaned over and kissed him. Billy Joe responded, hugged Carlos goodbye, and then let him go. "I'll see you tomorrow."

Billy Joe heard the words as though he had cotton in his ears. His thoughts were so very far away right now. He nodded and stood to walk Carlos to the door as though he were a robot. "Tomorrow."

Carlos patted him on the shoulder. "Wherever you've gone, don't stay there too long. It doesn't seem like it's a good place for you." He patted him on the shoulder again and left the apartment.

Billy Joe closed the door behind him. He had to agree. His past was not a good place to be, and he needed to try to keep it there. That was much easier said than done, especially if that past somehow managed to catch up with him.

"STOP WOOLGATHERING," Michael said with a smack on the shoulder. "What's got you so worried?" He flashed his usual crooked, stunning smile, tilting his head to the side like a cocker spaniel. The man was wicked and knew just how to pull him out of a funk.

"No puppy-dog looks. That isn't fair," Billy Joe countered.

"You aren't going to tell me about it, are you?" Michael was a talented electrician and a huge gossip. Telephone, telegraph, tell Michael—they all had the same effect. "Okay. Then I'll just have to make shit up because you are so everlastingly boring." Michael turned back to the spool of wiring they were pulling through the ceiling of the building being given a face-lift.

"Just thinking about the holiday tomorrow." Billy Joe was looking forward to having a day off with a little fun. "Carlos is cooking. What plans do you have?"

Michael shrugged and went back to the wiring, climbing the ladder to tug the new wire through the conduit. Billy Joe fed the wire off the spool, keeping it from getting twisted. "I'll spend the day with football."

"Alone?" Billy Joe asked.

"Yeah." Michael reached over his head into the ceiling, tugged gently, and pulled the wire through. "There it is."

"Why don't you come over tomorrow? Judging by what Carlos has said, there's going to be plenty of food. The guys will gather in my place to watch the games, and the rest will be at Carlos's."

"I don't want to crash someone else's dinner."

Billy Joe smiled, feeling a little more like himself than he'd been in the last few days. Maybe being nice to someone else really was the cure for feeling like crap. "You wouldn't be. Carlos does this every year, and he loves to cook… usually for an army." He unwound more wire until the pull stopped. "Is that it?"

"Yeah. We're through. Now just eight more lines to pull today." Michael was smiling again. "If you're serious, I'd love to come."

"Awesome." Billy Joe cut the wire, and they got ready to move their equipment. "Come by at about two, and don't let me forget to give you the address." It was nice making another friend—the next step in building a new life.

BILLY JOE and Michael finished the day, and then Billy Joe picked Tyler up at day care before heading home. Tyler talked about his day the entire ride. His energy was amazing, and it helped keep some of Billy Joe's doldrums at bay.

"I made a turkey for Mr. Carlos." Tyler held up the paper plate turkey covered in colorful paint.

"He's going to love it." Billy Joe swallowed hard and continued driving. He pulled into his parking space and helped Tyler out before going inside, dodging the rain and trying to keep Tyler out of the puddles.

Even the hallway smelled amazing as they hurried up to the apartment. "I'm hungry," Tyler said, turning toward Carlos's door. Tyler dashed over and knocked loudly. "He not home." Tyler pouted, and Billy Joe unlocked their door. Tyler ran inside and placed his turkey on the table.

"You can have a glass of milk and a cookie." Billy Joe took off his coat and hung it up, along with Tyler's, before getting the snack. They sat together at the table, Billy Joe with a beer.

"Why you sad?" Tyler asked. "No be sad no more." Tyler climbed off his chair and hurried around the table to climb onto Billy Joe's lap. "There. You no be sad."

"That's right. You're here, and I can't be sad any longer." Billy Joe hated the cloud that seemed to have settled over his spirit.

"Are Gran and Grampy coming for Thanksgiving?" Tyler looked up, and Billy Joe shook his head. "Don't they love me no more?"

Billy Joe hugged Tyler to his chest, not having a clue how to answer that question and not hurt Tyler more. "They love you, but they're a long ways away." He decided to try distraction. "We're going to have Thanksgiving with Carlos and some of his friends, as well as my friend from work. There will be lots of people and plenty of things to talk about. When you're done with your cookie and milk, why don't you draw a special Thanksgiving picture that we can put up with your turkey? It will make the party more festive if there are decorations."

"Will you help?" Tyler asked before taking his final bite of cookie.

"Sure. Drink your milk." Billy Joe lifted Tyler off his lap and placed him back in his seat. "I'll go get the crayons and paper." He went to the lower shelf of the linen closet, which he'd turned into a toy cabinet for Tyler, and got the box of crayons and a pad of drawing paper. He took them to Tyler, who was holding up his empty sippy cup. Billy Joe sat down next to him, and they started on their masterpieces.

A few minutes later, a knock startled them. Billy Joe checked who it was before opening the door. "Tyler and I were drawing decorations for tomorrow," he told Carlos as he came inside. Billy Joe kissed him, and they both sat at the table. "Is it okay if we have one more join us tomorrow? Michael was going to spend the day alone. I asked if he wanted to join us. I hope that's okay."

"It's great," Carlos answered right away, picking up a few crayons and starting a picture himself.

Billy Joe watched Tyler work, putting down his crayons. He was a terrible artist, so it seemed Tyler had inherited some talent from his mother.

"I drawed a turkey." Tyler grinned and held it up. Both Billy Joe and Carlos praised it. Billy Joe set the colorful drawing aside, and Tyler started a new one. "What's that?" Tyler asked Carlos as he worked.

"I'm drawing you," Carlos said with a smile.

Billy Joe leaned over, his eyes widening. The colors weren't true to life, but it was definitely Tyler, and as Carlos worked, the likeness grew more pronounced. "That's really good."

"I'm glad you like it."

Billy Joe stood, leaving the two of them to their coloring, and went to start something for dinner. He figured something simple would be good, given the huge meal they were going to have tomorrow.

"Pizza, Daddy," Tyler said, throwing his two cents into the ring.

"We had that two nights ago."

"Sketti," Tyler offered up.

Billy Joe found a box of pasta in the cupboard and some sauce that Carlos had made in his freezer. Over the last week or so, Carlos had taken to filling Billy Joe's freezer because his own was overflowing, apparently. "Okay." Billy Joe put water on and found some bread to make garlic toast.

"How was work?" Carlos asked, just as Billy Joe's phone rang.

He picked it up, staring wide-eyed and almost unable to breathe when he saw the number. He didn't recognize it specifically, but by the area code, he knew it was coming from Mississippi.

"What is it?" Carlos asked, and Billy Joe showed him the phone, which was still vibrating. Carlos took it and answered. "May I help you?" He waited and then hung up. "Clicks. I think it was telemarketers."

Billy Joe inhaled deeply to slow his racing heart. "Thank goodness." He felt the blood returning to his head and feet. "When I saw—"

"It's okay. Just relax."

"Was that Granny? I tried calling her." Tyler grinned and hurried off. He came running back in with his sweatshirt, pointing to the spot to put a name and phone number. Tyler was a smart boy, but damn, he'd have to keep his phone away from him. The last thing he wanted was for Tyler to call his parents and tell them where he was.

"On what?" Billy Joe kept his voice level.

"The phone." Tyler pointed to the plastic toy on the floor. "Can we call on the real one, Daddy?"

81

"Maybe soon," Billy Joe answered, scared to death that somehow his father was going to find him. He had no intention of ever speaking to him again. "Why don't you go back to your coloring while I make dinner?"

"Do you need help?" Carlos asked.

"No. You relax and have some fun."

Billy Joe finished making dinner, and by the time they were ready to eat, there were plenty of decorations for the following day. Carlos cleared off the table, and they all sat down for dinner.

"What's been bothering you these past few days?" Carlos asked. "And please don't tell me nothing. I've watched you stare blankly at the television for an hour without really seeing a thing. You're jumpy and…." Carlos set down the fork and spoon he was using to roll his spaghetti. "Is there something you want to tell me and can't figure out how?" He raised his eyebrows.

That was exactly it, and therein lay the problem. "I'm not sure…."

"If you just want to be friends, then…." Carlos stared at his plate.

"No," Billy Joe said quickly. "It isn't that." He rolled his eyes when Carlos smiled and sighed with what Billy Joe hoped was relief. "There's been a lot that's changed in the last few weeks, and I'm—"

"Does it have to do with your family? Did you get something other than the phone call to make you think they found you?"

Billy Joe shook his head. "You know I ran away from a pretty bad situation, and I'm trying not to let that interfere with my life here." God, he was skirting the issue something terrible, but he didn't want Carlos tainted by what he'd left behind. "Can you understand that I left them behind and I want things here to be happier?" Billy Joe was about to play the Tyler card when Carlos nodded and went back to eating, but he didn't say much, growing quiet for the rest of dinner. Once they were done and Billy Joe got Tyler cleaned up and settled with some toys on the floor, they sat together to watch a little television.

"I know you're keeping something from me," Carlos said. "Probably for the best reasons, but whatever it is, it's eating at you and making you scared and jumpy." He sighed, taking Billy Joe's hand. "You don't have to tell me until you're ready, but I don't like it. Whatever you're carrying around is hurting you."

Billy Joe was well aware of that. The last few nights, he'd had nightmares, and they were all about his last night in Mississippi. Billy Joe kept seeing what happened over and over again, like it was a never-ending movie where he couldn't get up and leave.

"I don't want to hurt you or Tyler." He had to keep this to himself so his family didn't know where he was or how to locate him. That was the only way they could all be safe, and Billy Joe would do just about anything to keep the ones he cared about from harm. He'd thought about telling Carlos what had happened, but each time he got close, he stopped himself, for Carlos's own good. What Billy Joe knew was going to cause a lot of people harm— people back home who didn't take that kind of thing lightly and made others pay for their hurts.

BILLY JOE was still unsettled when he woke the following morning to his phone chiming that he had a message. It was from Carlos.

Can you come over? I need some help.

Billy Joe got out of bed and pulled on some sweatpants, a sweatshirt, and socks before padding quietly across the hall. Maybe what he needed was to get a baby monitor so he could listen in case Tyler needed him when he was over at Carlos's.

"What's going on? It's only six in the morning," Billy Joe said quietly as Carlos opened the door and ushered him inside. He inhaled, the scent of food already permeating the apartment.

"It's too early to put the turkey in the oven," Carlos said, "but I was getting it ready and—" He leaned close. "—I realized I missed you." He put his arms around Billy Joe's neck and drew him in, their lips finding each other's even in the dim light drifting out from the kitchen.

Billy Joe forgot about the fact that he hadn't slept but a few hours because every time he did, the damn nightmares started up again. He also forgot about his worries and everyone back in Mississippi. Hell, after two seconds, he forgot his own damn name, with Carlos kissing him as though he were the very center of the universe. Billy Joe threw himself into the kiss, letting go of everything except the amazement of how a man like Carlos— educated, caring, smart, funny—could be interested in him.

"Is this what you called me for?" Billy Joe asked when they broke apart.

"Is that bad?"

Billy Joe grinned. "God, no." He kissed Carlos once again, wishing he could take him into the bedroom and give them both something to be thankful for.

"Billy Joe…."

Billy Joe sighed. "Tyler is asleep, but I can't leave him alone for very long." His entire body quivered with anticipation. He wanted Carlos as badly as he'd wanted anything or anyone in his life.

"I know. It's just that we never get any time to spend alone." Carlos sighed. "I understand, and… forget I said anything. Tyler has to come first." He looked up, smiling. "Maybe we could see if he wants to have a sleepover tonight. We could build him a tent in the spare room and he could have an inside campout."

Billy Joe got the idea loud and clear. Tyler could go "camping," and his daddy could have a sleepover of his own. He liked that idea. "We'll ask him when he gets up." Billy Joe kissed Carlos once again, hoping like hell his hard-on wasn't as obvious as he was afraid it was. Thankfully, a glance down confirmed that Carlos was just as excited. At least he wasn't the only one frustrated. Billy Joe tugged Carlos closer, rubbing against him, delight arching through him as he clung to him. He was seconds away from losing control and forced himself back from the edge. "Sorry." Billy Joe pulled away.

"God." Carlos was breathing like a sprinter, his eyes wide, pupils dilated. It was sexy as hell.

"I know." Something had to change, and not just because he was horny and wanted Carlos. Billy Joe was quickly relying on Carlos for a lot, and it scared him. It wasn't just his body that ached for Carlos—his heart wanted him, needed some one-on-one time, some quiet time, for just the two of them. "I need to get back. When Tyler gets up, we'll come over and help with dinner and stuff."

"Cool." Carlos swallowed and nodded. "You better go. I need a few minutes to calm down."

Billy Joe understood that situation. He went back across the hall and closed the door. He decided on a shower to try to cool himself off. By then Tyler would be up and he'd need breakfast.

"WHEN DO we eat?" Tyler asked for the fourth time. He sat at the table, pulling some grapes off stems and putting them in a bowl.

"Don't eat all the grapes," Billy Joe told Tyler as he put yet another one in his mouth. "You're supposed to be helping, not eating." He ruffled Tyler's hair, returning to peeling and cutting up the potatoes.

"Guests will arrive in half an hour, and we're almost done." Carlos put a casserole dish in the oven with the turkey, and the scents wafting out smelled divine.

"Yummy," Tyler said as he finished his task. "Can I watch TV?" He climbed down, and Billy Joe got him settled with a sippy cup of milk. Then Billy Joe put the grapes away, finished his potatoes, and set the large pot on the stove. Carlos had everything timed and was starting the potatoes soon.

Carlos went across the hall to check on what was in the oven there, closing the door. When he returned, a couple was with him. "Billy Joe, Tyler, this is Angie and Andy Hofstadter. Angie works with me in the library, and Andy is a supervisor at one of the contract warehouses in the area. Billy Joe just joined the maintenance staff at the university."

Billy Joe shook hands with them both. "This is my son, Tyler."

Tyler was suddenly very shy until Angie knelt down and presented him with a coloring book and fresh crayons. "Oh, thank you!" he said, clutching the book adorably to his chest, and grinned a huge grin.

"You're welcome, sweetheart," Angie said, and Tyler raced over to the coffee table and knelt on the floor to start coloring. "Carlos has told me a lot about you." Angie hugged Billy Joe enthusiastically. "It's so good to meet you."

"He talks about you guys all the time too." Billy Joe stepped back so they could get by him.

"The game is starting soon," Andy pronounced, heading for the television. Billy Joe shared a smirk with Carlos. Andy was going to have a fight on his hands if he thought Tyler was going to give up Dora. "Tyler, do you like football?"

Tyler turned to Andy like he'd grown a second head. "No. Dora," he said firmly, coloring and watching the show.

"Little dude, Thanksgiving is football day." Andy pouted.

"Sweetheart," Angie said, "Billy Joe's apartment is right across the hall. After dinner, you can go on over and yell to your heart's content."

"Michael, one of the guys I work with, is coming too, and I suspect the two of you can talk football all you like."

Andy smiled. "Awesome."

Angie helped Carlos in the kitchen. Billy Joe was on drink duty and made sure everyone had something.

Marie from the circulation desk arrived. She was in her early fifties, had bright eyes, graying hair, and a quick laugh that Billy Joe liked. Apparently she and Andy were football buddies. They started in on the prospects for Penn State almost before the door closed.

"How long have you worked at the library?" Billy Joe asked when he could get a word in.

She snorted softly, which made him smile. "I swear we used to handwrite the books in my day." Her smile turned to a grin. "Now everything is electronic this and digital that. I love that there is so much information available, but I had a freshman ask me last week why we had paper magazines. She looked down her nose at me. 'No one reads those anymore....' You know the put-upon, know-it-all tone. As soon as she said it, three students grabbed magazines off the rack right in front of her, and I had to bite my lip to keep from laughing."

"How did she think they read magazines?" Billy Joe asked.

Marie sighed. "These kids think if they read the crap on Facebook or whatever social media site is popular in the moment, that they're well informed about the world, which is ridiculous." She sighed again.

Billy Joe got her a drink. He wasn't big into Facebook or Twitter and stuff. "I like magazines," he told her when he brought her a glass of white wine.

"Don't pay any attention to me. I'm an old fart who doesn't want to see things like print books and magazines go the way of the vinyl record. Some things are sacred." She sipped from her glass. "Oh, did I tell you guys the latest?" she asked Angie and Carlos. "I had a student bring up a copy of one of the European news magazines. We carry some from most countries. She was appalled."

"I don't understand," Billy Joe said, looking to Carlos.

"They regularly have covers that are more risqué than they are here. Often with a naked woman. It's no big deal to them, and the covers are artistic rather than porny...."

"I see."

"She asked me why we didn't cover them up with Post-it notes or something." Her eyes sparkled. Marie was clearly having fun with this.

"What did you do? The library has policies about censorship," Angie interjected as she carried a salad bowl to the table.

"I asked her if she was suggesting that we put pasties on the covers. I kept my voice even. 'We don't censor things here,' I added quickly. 'This is about freedom of ideas and expression.' I encouraged her to look beyond the cover." Marie emptied her glass, and Billy Joe got her some more wine. He hoped she didn't drink like that the entire afternoon or she'd be drunk off her ass.

"What did she say?" Billy Joe stood and went to the door to answer the knock, listening to Marie as he went.

"Nothing, thank goodness. I'm so tired of the sanctimonious and self-righteous."

Billy Joe laughed as he opened the door. "Hey, Michael. Glad you can make it."

"Thanks for the invite." Michael pressed a bottle of white wine into his hands, and Billy Joe made introductions. "Hey, all."

Carlos set snacks on the coffee table, and everyone got to talking. Billy Joe checked with Carlos about the food, and Carlos set him to mashing the potatoes while he went across the hall. Thankfully Tyler's program had ended, and they turned off the television to cut down on the noise.

"Daddy...." Tyler tugged on his pant leg. "Look at my colors." He held up the book, and Billy Joe looked at the pages. They were pretty good. He tended to stay within the lines for the most part, which was awesome. His use of color was interesting, however.

"Go show Miss Angie," Billy Joe said, and Tyler hurried over to her. She was a good sport, praising Tyler's work and helping him color another picture.

"We should be ready in about ten minutes," Carlos said.

Billy Joe finished the potatoes, leaving them in the pan to stay warm while Carlos got the turkey out of the oven. The next few minutes were a blur of activity as final preparations were finished and all the food brought to the table.

"Hey, Billy Joe," Michael said, calling him over. "Tyler wanted to call his gran and grampy. He showed me the number, and I dialed it but figured I should ask first, but…. Oh shit."

"Granny," Tyler exclaimed as he held Michael's phone. The rest was Tyler talking so fast, Billy Joe could barely understand it. Clearly Tyler was excited.

Billy Joe wondered what in the hell he should do. Ending the call was going to make Tyler really upset. At least it wasn't his phone, so his parents wouldn't have his number, but they would know roughly where he was from the number.

"What is it?" Carlos asked softly from behind him. Billy Joe hadn't even heard him approach as near-panic rose, threatening to cut off his ability to think at all. "Who is Tyler on the phone with?"

"Michael called my mom for him." Billy Joe's hand shook. He needed to think.

"Daddy!" Tyler ran over and handed him the phone.

Billy Joe took it, looking at it like the phone was going to explode any second. "Hello," he said quietly, hoping to hell his father had already hung up.

"What the hell do you think you're doing? I have the police out looking for you and Tyler," his father screamed in his ear. "You get your ass in the car and back here right the fuck now! What do you think you're doing?"

"No," Billy Joe said softly, shame building as his insides quivered. "I left because I don't want Tyler around you any longer. I want him to have a better life than the piece-of-shit one you gave me." He shook from head to toe. Everyone in the room stared at him, and Billy Joe nearly dropped the phone.

"I've brought charges for kidnapping with the sheriff," his father said.

"You can't. He's my son, and you might have the sheriff in your white-sheeted pocket, but that won't go anywhere. I have his birth certificate with me and can prove he's my son." Billy Joe inhaled deeply, his arms and legs tingling.

Carlos put his hand on his shoulder, and when Billy Joe turned, he took the phone. "I don't know what you think you're pulling. But you have no power here," Carlos growled into the line.

Billy Joe managed to catch his breath. He lifted Tyler into his arms and carried him out of the apartment and across the hall. Tyler was crying, probably not sure what had happened but aware Billy Joe was upset.

"It's okay, Tyler." Billy Joe held him close, sitting on their sofa in the quiet room.

"Why you yell at Grampy?" Tyler hugged him in return. "I tell him Happy Thanksgiving."

Billy Joe closed his eyes and gently rocked Tyler slowly from side to side. "I know you only wanted to say hello." God, he hadn't counted on Tyler asking someone else to call and them actually doing it. That seemed so strange.

There was a knock and then Michael stuck his head in. "I'm sorry, man. I didn't know, and when he asked to call his gran, I thought I was going to make the kid happy." Michael came inside, his hands in his pockets. "I really am sorry."

"It's all right." At least they hadn't called on his phone and his father didn't know whose phone it was. "I didn't want them to know where I was...."

Michael grinned. "Dude, my phone number is from when I lived in Michigan. If they have the number, they'll get the info for my mom and dad. It's on their account so we get a bigger family discount." Michael must have gotten his phone back from Carlos, because it rang, and he pulled it out of his pocket. "Dang, that guy is persistent." He unlocked the phone and showed it to Billy Joe, declined the call, and went into the settings. "I blocked the number."

"Thanks, but...." Billy Joe was pretty sure that the damage had been done.

Carlos hurried in. "Your dad hung up on me." He seemed proud of it. "Can I ask you something? The number Tyler has for your dad—is it their home number or a cell phone?"

"What's Grampy's phone number?" Billy Joe asked, and Tyler ran to get his sweatshirt and showed him. "Thank God," he whispered softly. "The phone is one of those wall-hung things with the long cord. It's what my mom likes, and it doesn't have a display." He put Tyler down and slowly got to his feet.

"Then you don't have anything to worry about. Your father demanded that I tell him where you were, and of course I told him to go to hell. I do think he's serious about calling the police down there."

"You might think about contacting them just to say that you left of your own free will and that you took your son," Michael offered, but Billy Joe shook his head, pleading silently with Carlos.

"Let's everyone go back inside to dinner. The excitement is over and everything is on the table." Carlos ushered everyone out, taking Tyler's hand.

"Daddy...," Tyler said when Billy Joe stayed put. He didn't feel much like Thanksgiving, or eating at all for that matter. He inhaled deeply, sighed, and figured he could put on a brave face for Tyler and Carlos. He didn't want to be a downer on the holiday.

Billy Joe ended up sitting in the seat at one end, near Carlos, with Tyler next to him.

"Thank you all for coming." Carlos slid his hand across the tablecloth to take Billy Joe's hand. "We have plenty to be thankful for, friends old and new." Carlos squeezed his fingers as he glanced at him. "Whatever our struggles throughout the year, today we remember what is good and happy in our lives." He gave his hand another squeeze, and Billy Joe's chest warmed, knowing he was one of the things Carlos was thankful for. Carlos lifted a wineglass in his other hand, and everyone around the table did the same. Tyler picked up his sippy cup. Everyone clinked glasses and then sipped.

"Can we eat now?" Tyler asked, and everyone chuckled.

Billy Joe smiled and tickled Tyler gently. "Yes. We can eat."

Carlos started serving turkey, passing plates around the table, with others dishing up the hot side dishes as the plates passed. As soon as Tyler got his plate, he dug in, the earlier drama quickly forgotten. Billy Joe wished he could let it go so easily.

"It's all right. Your father isn't going to find you," Carlos whispered. "Not from one phone call."

Billy Joe hoped he was right. He glanced in Carlos's direction and saw a ton of questions running across Carlos's gaze, but he didn't say anything. Thank goodness. Billy Joe knew he was going to have some explaining to do. He realized what he'd said on the phone and that Carlos was likely to have picked up on it.

"Where is your accent from?" Marie asked, her question cutting through Billy Joe's thoughts.

"Jackson, Mississippi," Billy Joe answered. "It's where I was raised. I think it's a nice city, with the university and all. Not that I spent too much time by the campus." His father talked about that part of town as though it were inhabited by lepers. Well, to his father, liberals and lepers were damn near the same thing.

"Why did you leave, then? Does it have to do with that phone call?" Marie ate a bite of potatoes.

"In a way, ma'am. My family is… very… conservative, and they were never in a million years going to accept that I was gay." There, he'd said it out loud again. "That was my father on the phone, and he…." Billy Joe turned to Carlos, hoping for some help.

"Billy Joe's father is an…." Carlos stopped, looking at Tyler. Billy Joe did the same thing. "He's not a nice man, at least not to me." He mouthed the word *asshole*. "Of the highest order. I talked to him for less than sixty seconds and I feel like I should take a shower." He shivered, and Billy Joe was thankful Tyler didn't seem to be paying attention. Billy Joe didn't want to say bad things about his mother and father in front of him.

"I see," Angie said. "I love my parents, but sometimes I'm so happy with the family I've chosen." She leaned against Andy's shoulder and smiled at Carlos.

"You can't pick your family, so thank God you can choose your friends," Michael said, to a chorus of agreement and plenty of nodding.

Billy Joe figured that truer words were never spoken.

"Is your dinner good?" Billy Joe asked Tyler. He'd eaten his potatoes and some of the stuffing, as well as a few bites of turkey, and it seemed as many olives as he could get his hands on. Billy Joe put a few more on his plate, and Tyler chomped them with a grin and nodded. "Then eat some more turkey and potatoes, and I'll give you a few more olives." How many soon-to-be three-year-olds loved olives?

"Tyler seems advanced for his age," Marie said. "He talks very well, and he colors like a kid a few years older. Have you had him tested?" She and Tyler made faces at each other for a second.

"Not yet. We've just gotten through the last of potty training, which was a major hurdle. He wasn't interested until he got to day care. Now he wants to be a big boy all the time. I'll talk to the folks at day care and see what they say." Billy Joe wasn't sure how to do a lot of this stuff. Mostly he was trying to make it through each day.

"Don't worry," Angie told him. "I know a lot of the professors and the people at the day care. I can refer you." She grinned. "After all, it looks like Andy and I are going to be needing them eventually."

"Oh my God, are you pregnant?" Carlos practically bounced off his chair.

"I just found out. Hence the water."

"That's great." Billy Joe smiled as he shared in the collective joy.

"Were you happy when I was pregnant?" Tyler asked, and Billy Joe had to bite his lip to keep from laughing.

"Yes. I was happy when I found out your mom was pregnant and I was going to have you." That wasn't necessarily true. Billy Joe had been scared to death, and there had been weeks of uncertainty and plenty of ups and downs, but as soon as he'd held Tyler in the hospital and those eyes looked at him for the first time, he'd known he'd do anything for the little bundle in his arms.

"Can I see the baby?" Tyler asked.

"It's inside her, growing in her belly. That's what being pregnant means."

Tyler's mouth hung open. "She has a baby in her belly?"

Billy Joe nodded, and he could see Tyler processing the information.

"But where does it fit?" He jumped off his seat and ran around to Angie, looking at her belly.

Angie chuckled. "It's just small right now, but the baby will get bigger and my belly will get bigger." She took Tyler's hand and placed it on her tummy. "Eventually the baby will even kick and stuff."

"Daddy...." Tyler laughed.

Billy Joe nodded. "Come back and finish your dinner," he reminded Tyler, and Tyler returned to his seat. He ate a little bit more before declaring he was full and asking if he could watch Dora. Billy Joe got him set up in front of the television with the volume low, then returned to the table.

Carlos, Marie, and Angie talked about the library and gossiped, while Michael and Andy talked football. Billy Joe didn't have much to add to either conversation, so he listened and began clearing the table. It gave him something to do.

"I have pie for dessert," Carlos said as he helped with the last of the dishes. "We can have that a little later if you like."

"Michael, football?" Andy asked, and they headed across the hall. The others settled around the room. Tyler was getting tired, so Billy Joe took him into Carlos's second bedroom and laid him on the love seat in there for a nap. He put a blanket over him, and Tyler was completely out. Billy Joe left the door cracked open and joined the others in the living room.

Most people had their feet up. They found a movie to watch and seemed to sink into a turkey hangover. Carlos refilled drink glasses, and they watched *The Wedding Date* and talked softly so as not to wake Tyler.

"Why Pennsylvania?" Marie asked at one point. "Why stop here?"

Billy Joe chuckled slightly. "It's where I had car trouble. Carlos helped me." He told them the story of the early snowstorm. "He was so nice, and I was...." God, he tried to think of something to say that didn't make him sound like a complete loser.

"Billy Joe was a little out of his element. I mean, how much snow do they get down there? And it was coming down hard. I couldn't leave them out in that mess." Carlos bumped his shoulder.

"You didn't plan on coming here, then?" Marie asked, like a dog with a bone.

"No. I wasn't sure where I was going. All I wanted was to get as far away from my family as I could." Billy Joe closed his eyes, trying not to think of the reason. He was afraid Marie would try to pull that bit of information out of him as well. He was keeping that to himself, held deep down... for all their sakes.

"There's more there, I just know it." She smiled and leaned forward to pat Billy Joe's knee. "I'd love to hear it when you're ready to tell it someday."

Billy Joe knew he should say nothing, but his mouth was already engaged. "Why do you think that?"

Marie got up from the chair and sat next to him on the sofa. "People don't just leave their home and everything they know on a whim. Lots of folks do it for a job, but you already said you didn't have a destination in mind. Throughout history, people have migrated for a number of reasons—famine, crop failure, industrial collapse, and so on. But they don't generally leave home and the only life they ever knew, with a son no less, on a whim. Something bad happened, and it probably involved your father." She lightly touched his shoulder. "Like I said, when you're ready to tell the story, I would love to hear it." She leaned closer. "And let me know if you need help." Her voice was just above a whisper and as gentle as a spring breeze. "I know what fear looks like. I've been there in my life as well. My husband was a real son of a bitch, and I lived in fear for a long time until I had help to get out." She patted his shoulder once again. "You have nothing to fear from me, and I'm glad you met Carlos. He's a special person, and I hope you make each other happy."

Billy Joe expected the "if you hurt him" speech, but he figured that was probably implied. He was sure Marie could be a real ballbuster when she chose to. "Thanks." What else could he say to something like that?

Marie patted his shoulder once again, then pulled her hand away. "I love this scene," she said, turning her attention to the dance lesson in the movie where Debra Messing stomped Dermot Mulroney's foot and he proceeded to sweep her off her feet. "I used to love to go dancing." She cleared her throat and turned away from the television, then asked Carlos if he minded if she turned off the television.

Carlos switched it off and turned on some music and went back to talking to Angie.

"It's so exciting," Marie said, entering the baby conversation.

"Andy and I have been trying for a long time, and I didn't think we were going to be able to conceive. I have problems… but once I stopped worrying and he and I decided we were going to try adopting…." She smiled as she touched her belly. "Something more to be thankful for." She grinned, and Billy Joe's heart warmed for her. The greatest joy in his life was Tyler, so he knew some of what she felt.

Carlos jumped up and turned the music a little louder. Then he hurried over, holding his hand out to Angie. She took it, and the two of them started dancing. Billy Joe pushed the coffee table to the side and then asked Marie. She refused at first, but then took his hand, and Billy Joe led her around the living room. The song ended, and Andy came over from the other apartment. He cut in, dancing with his wife, and Marie spun Billy Joe into Carlos.

The music slowed, and Billy Joe moved in close, resting his head on Carlos's shoulder. He clutched him, trying to let go of what he'd driven a thousand miles to leave behind, but it seemed to keep catching up with him. Billy Joe realized now that he could drive as far as he wanted, but he wasn't going to be able to run from his own thoughts and what he'd seen. That, he would carry with him forever. No matter what he did, Billy Joe couldn't outrun his own thoughts.

"It's my fault," Billy Joe mumbled under his breath.

"What? You haven't done anything," Carlos whispered back.

Billy Joe clamped his eyes closed, holding Carlos tighter. He didn't answer because he didn't want to go there. But this was all his fault, all of it. And he could drive to the end of the earth and it would change nothing. What had happened was because of him.

"Daddy, I wanna dance too," Tyler said as he came back in the living room, rubbing his eyes.

Carlos stepped back slightly, presumably to give Tyler room, but Tyler seemed content to do his own dance, and Billy Joe clung to Carlos like a lifeline, wondering what the hell he was going to do.

CHAPTER 6

THE REST of Thanksgiving was awesome, except for that damned phone call. For most of the day, every time Carlos had touched or even looked at Billy Joe, a low-wattage tingling zipped through him, like when he'd stuck his tongue to a battery as a kid. Even now he could feel it, sitting in the second bedroom under a sheet draped between the sofa and the desk, knowing Billy Joe was just outside waiting for him.

Carlos had a sleeping bag from when he was a kid that he used as a couch blanket in the winter. He'd zipped it up and settled Tyler with a pillow and a flashlight. They had turned off all the lights, and Tyler had insisted that Carlos read *The Velveteen Rabbit*. It was supposed to settle Tyler to sleep, but it wasn't working.

"Close your eyes and I'll read you *Clifford*, and then you go to sleep. Okay?" Carlos set the first book aside and picked up the second. This one seemed to have the desired effect, and by the time he was done, Tyler was asleep. Carlos climbed out of the tent, left the room, and closed the door.

"Is he out?" Billy Joe asked as Carlos approached.

"Yeah. He's finally asleep. I think he was so overstimulated with everything that happened today that he didn't want it to end." Carlos sank down on the sofa. "He asked me if we were having Thanksgiving next week too." He grinned. "I told him that it was once a year and that next month it was Christmas."

"He barely remembers that from last year. Mom and Dad gave him a few presents, and I got him what I could. It wasn't much, and he didn't really understand and barely sat still to open his presents." Billy Joe sat down next to Carlos. "My dad bought Tyler a gun. It wasn't real, but the dang thing looked it."

"Was it a squirt gun or something?" Carlos took Billy Joe's hand, that tingling having shifted to concern.

"Bubbles. But it gave me the creeps, and as soon as we were done opening presents, Dad took Tyler outside to play bubbles. Tyler would blow bubbles with the thing, and my dad would pretend to be shot." Billy Joe quivered. "It was sick, and my mother went along with it. She actually told me that Tyler needed to learn about protecting our second amendment rights. He was two! I hid the damn thing as soon as Christmas was over, and when Dad wasn't around, I smashed it and threw the whole thing away." Billy Joe groaned and leaned back. His eyes had bags under them.

"You need to get some rest." Carlos was tired as well.

"Yeah, I probably do." Billy Joe seemed to be waiting. He took a deep breath. "I guess I owe you an explanation about my father."

Carlos had been curious. Billy Joe's comment about white-sheeted pockets hadn't gone unnoticed. "I think you need to tell me what's going on."

Billy Joe nodded. "You probably guessed something of what I'm going to tell you. My dad leads a local white supremacist group. I grew up with it. My dad joined before he was married, and my mom's dad was a member too. So that shit is a family tradition. Dad believes all that stuff, hook, line, and sinker." He paused. "I had to get out."

"I understand. If your dad knew you were gay, he'd...." Carlos trailed off, not knowing how to finish that sentence.

"My dad would kill me. Literally. He'd take Tyler away, then drag me out somewhere and put me down like a rabid dog." Billy Joe shook, and Carlos put his arms around him, doing his best to comfort him. "I know you think I'm exaggerating, but I'm not. I know he would because I saw him do it."

Carlos went cold from head to toe. He had to have heard that wrong. "Billy Joe...."

"No. I have to say this before I chicken out again. I saw it. My dad and his buddies were out at one of their gatherings. I knew Dad was going, and Mom had Tyler. I said I was going into town to meet some friends. But I heard where the gathering was and I knew a place I could park, so I went out there. I didn't realize it was some big local gathering, but there were all kinds of people there. Dad and some other men spoke to get everyone riled up, and then they brought out someone. I didn't recognize him at first, but it was Hilliard. They had him tied up and gagged, kneeling in front of my dad. I know he had to be scared shitless, and then my dad started speaking about gay people being the dogs of humanity that needed to be put down… and one of the men did just that. They shot him in the head." Billy Joe buried his face in Carlos's side, crying. Carlos held him as his shirt grew damp. "My dad stood there and had someone kill Hilliard." Billy Joe shook hard, and Carlos felt tears welling in his own eyes.

"Oh my God…." His breath came in short gasps. "You saw it?"

"Yeah. I got the hell out of there after that, back to my car. I heard them still chanting and yelling, so I hoped I was safe. I decided on my way back to Mom and Dad's that I had to get out of there. I shopped for stuff, filled the back with supplies, packed in secret, and after everyone was asleep, took off with Tyler." Billy Joe's breath came in short pants. Carlos rubbed his back, talking softly to try to get him to relax.

"It's okay. You need to calm down. He's in another area of the country and he can't hurt you." Carlos soothed small circles on Billy Joe's back.

"I can't. It's my fault." Billy Joe wiped his eyes, but more tears streamed down his cheeks. "I had gone to see Hilliard a week or so before I left. One of my dad's buddies, Sniffs, the guy is a tracker. He walked up to the table to say hi, and I nearly panicked. He said hello, and I introduced Hilliard like we were just friends. But who knows what happened afterward. Maybe Sniffs followed him, or maybe he was in the wrong place at the wrong time. I don't know. But what if I put Hilliard on their radar?" Billy Joe groaned. "I don't know anything anymore. My friend, the one who helped me, is gone, and I saw him get murdered." Billy Joe wiped his eyes again, turning away, and then leaned forward, holding his head. "What if he saved my life and I cost Hilliard his?"

"You don't know what happened. And all you can deal with is what you saw. Do you know who actually pulled the trigger?"

Billy Joe nodded. "I know just about everyone who was there. They weren't wearing hoods or anything because they probably thought they were out far enough that no one was going to bother them. People don't go there because of the stuff that happens there. They've basically put the fear of God into everyone. Those people are nuts."

"But you lived it," Carlos said, trying to get his mind around everything that he was being told. He knew Billy Joe had a shit family and bad childhood, but he was just figuring out how bad it was.

"Yes. Every day of my life. I used to hear my dad swearing when I was a kid. That name I called the lady at the grocery store was nothing compared to the crap that came out of my dad's mouth every day of my life. I was always ashamed of him for that, and scared at the same time." Billy Joe turned to Carlos. "Do you have any idea what it's like to live in total fear for a decade? I knew I was different. Being gay is hard, but being gay in a white supremacist family is impossible. I had to hide everything about who I was. Dad used to take me to rallies. People would be protesting, and I used to always look away from them, afraid someone would see that I belonged over there." Billy Joe stood, went to the kitchen, returned with a glass of water, and drank hastily. He set the empty glass on the coffee table. "The things I did just to try to fit in...." He shivered. "I don't want to think about how many people I hurt because I didn't have the guts to stand up for them. That changed with Hilliard. He showed me that I was stronger than I realized and that I could have pride in who I was."

Carlos stood as well. "Regardless of what happened or how they got hold of him, you aren't responsible for what happened to Hilliard. The men who brought him out there are. And the man who shot him is guilty of murder. Not you." He hugged Billy Joe even as he thought about what their next steps were. "You need to write down everything you know: names, places, everything."

Billy Joe paled and shook his head. "I just want to forget all of it... I have to."

"You want to let off whoever killed your friend, Hilliard, the man you say saved your life?" Carlos pulled away. "I know you're scared, but is that really what you want?" He thought Billy Joe was a better person than that.

"Of course not. I want that asshole to go to jail and rot there. But it isn't going to happen. He'll have an airtight alibi—they all will. Every single person at that rally will have someone who will vouch that they were someplace else. You have to understand that. I've seen my dad arrange it. All it takes is a phone call. 'I was with you last Thursday. You remember, right?'" Billy Joe began pacing again, his hands shaking. "Suddenly my dad is on the other side of the county or in Alabama."

"You really want them to get away with this?" Carlos's mouth hung open. "I can't believe it." He went into the kitchen, needing to do something with his hands or he was going to punch something.

"I need Tyler to be safe. That's what has to happen. It's why I left and came here."

"But your dad doesn't know you were there," Carlos said, picking up a dish towel. "Just call and leave a tip. Tell what you saw and let law enforcement take it from there. They have to be looking for Hilliard, and if you tell them where they might be able to find him, they'll find he was shot and can go from there."

Billy Joe shook his head. "I tried that already. They aren't going to find him. Someone probably wrapped him in a tarp and dumped him in a bayou on the way home. He was most likely alligator food long ago and there isn't anything left." Billy Joe's voice cracked. He sat down, shivering slightly, and Carlos set the dishes aside. "I want to help, but I need to be safe too."

Carlos thought for a few seconds, fear palpable in the room. "Just write down what you saw. I'll help you if you want. I know you want Hilliard to have justice." He sighed. "Think about it. What if they do that to someone else and you could stop it?" Damn, he was putting a lot of pressure on Billy Joe, but this couldn't just be allowed to drop.

"I know. But...."

Carlos came up behind Billy Joe and slid his arms around his waist. "What would your dad do in this kind of situation?"

Billy Joe stiffened, tension filling him.

"Then do the opposite."

"Yeah. Okay. If you'll help me, I'll write down everything that I saw and all the people I recognized. There isn't going to be any way to come back from this. People who cross the group get killed." Billy Joe was serious.

"We'll write it down and then figure out what to do with it. Okay? You can't let your dad and his cronies get away with this. You just can't." Carlos practically pleaded. "But I can't...." His words tapered off. "I can't tell you what to do." He backed away once again, trying to keep the disappointment out of his voice. Yes, he knew fear, but not the kind Billy Joe had described, and from his expression, that fear ruled pretty heavily at the moment. "I'm sorry for thinking I can dictate what you need to do or that I can somehow be your conscience." He swallowed hard. "Only you can decide what's right for you and Tyler."

Billy Joe shook his head. "No. I will write down what I saw and who I saw there. I don't know what I'll do with it yet, but...." He slumped against him. "I have to keep Tyler safe from him. Someone like that can't have influence over him, trying to shape the way he sees the world. I cannot bear the thought of my father coloring Tyler's world in any way, shape, or form."

Billy Joe stepped away, went to the bedroom door, and looked inside. He stayed where he was for a while, just watching his son. Carlos wanted to try to comfort him. He thought Billy Joe needed a chance to work things through for himself.

Carlos finished cleaning up the kitchen. He needed to give Billy Joe time. Once all the dishes were done and the counters wiped down, he left the dishrag over the faucet to dry and returned to the living room.

Billy Joe still stood in the doorway, head bowed forward, shoulders slumped. Carlos couldn't leave him looking so beaten down. He slowly went to him and touched Billy Joe's shoulder gently. Billy Joe didn't turn around, but continued watching Tyler sleep.

"I need to know that he'll be safe. That's all I want more than anything."

"I know, and he will be."

Billy Joe nodded. "Even he tells me Grampy is grumpy sometimes, and—" Billy Joe closed the bedroom door until just a crack remained. "—I can't let him have any more influence over him. Tyler is a smart little boy, and he deserves to grow up to his full potential, not have his head filled with backward thinking." He sighed and turned around. "If it hadn't been for him, I don't think I would have had the courage to leave."

Carlos tightened his hug, bringing him closer until their chests touched. "Is that really true?" He looked deeply into Billy Joe's eyes. "Don't sell yourself short. You weren't happy there and hadn't been for a while. Hiding who you are really sucks, and it's the most tiring thing I know. It weighs on the spirit until there's nothing left." He brought his lips up to touch Billy Joe's lightly.

"I suppose I owe it to Hilliard to do this." The sadness in Billy Joe's eyes was so deep that Carlos could feel it through him. "I owe it to Tyler…."

"And to yourself," Carlos whispered.

Billy Joe nodded and didn't pull away. "I do. I owe it to justice, and if I do this and see it through, maybe I can stop being afraid every time the phone rings or the doorbell sounds. I know I'm far away, but I still expect to see them outside." He sighed. "My dad said that he had called the police."

"Yes. Let's look up the number for the Jackson police. We can call them through the internet. They might be able to trace the call back to an IP address, but not to a phone number that your parents can call you at. That should give you some protection." Carlos wondered how they could be completely anonymous, but that was nearly impossible these days.

Billy Joe nodded. "I guess we have to. No sense waiting. I don't want someone here reacting to the complaint."

"No." Carlos went into his bedroom to retrieve his laptop. He'd taken it out of the spare room so Tyler wouldn't have any flashing lights bothering him while he was sleeping. Carlos brought up the website for the police department and then activated Skype.

The phone rang through the speaker and was then answered. Carlos motioned to Billy Joe, who looked like a deer caught in headlights. "Good evening." Carlos wasn't sure how to start. "I am here with a friend, and because of family issues, he and his son have left Mississippi."

"Yes, sir. How may I help you?" the operator said calmly.

"He spoke with his father today and was informed that his father had reported him missing. This wasn't a pleasant conversation, mostly yelling," Carlos explained.

"Can your friend speak for himself?" he asked in a thick, resonant bayou accent, a lot like Billy Joe's.

"Yes, sir," Billy Joe answered. "I'm calling to find out if my father, Clyde Massier, made a missing persons report. If he did, then I wish to state that I am not missing and left of my own accord and do not intend to return. I took my son with me—"

"And do you have custody of this child?" he asked.

"Yes, sir, though my father likes to think he calls the shots for everyone." Billy Joe had found his voice. "I do not want my father to know where I am under any circumstances, so I will not tell you where I am other than to say that I am in a completely different area of the country, where my son is safe." Billy Joe's hand shook and Carlos held it.

"You're doing just fine," Carlos said.

"All right, can you please tell me your name?"

"William Joseph Massier. My son is Tyler Massier." Billy Joe seemed a little more relaxed.

The officer took a minute, and Billy Joe's right leg bounced nervously. Carlos squeezed his hand once again. "I see a missing persons report was indeed made a few weeks ago through the sheriff's department. Are you saying that is incorrect?"

"Yes. I am not missing and left of my own free will. I called so that can be closed. I have given you my name and my son's name. But I will not send you a copy of my new driver's license because I don't want anyone there to know where I am." Billy Joe took a deep breath. He probably would have sent them a copy of his Mississippi license, but that had been surrendered when he got his new one.

"Why is that, sir?" the officer asked, suspicion ringing in his voice.

"Because my father has contacts through a lot of circles in Jackson, including law enforcement, and I don't know who I can trust. I'm calling so you aren't trying to find me and they can stop looking. I have spoken to my father today so he knows I left on my own. You have a good day." Billy Joe ended the call and sat back.

"Okay. That's enough to get them to end that," Carlos said.

"Won't they need proof?" Billy Joe asked. "I mean, they'll just take my word for it?"

Carlos shrugged. "You called them to say that you weren't actually missing, like your father reported. You gave his name, as well as yours and Tyler's. They're going to want to close the case anyway because there are never enough resources. So your call will get passed on and that will be the end of it. The police will probably close everything out and be done with it." Carlos sighed. "Why don't we call it a night? You've had just about all the excitement I think anyone can stand for one Thanksgiving."

"You got that right." Billy Joe looked like he'd been through a wringer.

Carlos took his hand, leading him toward the bedroom.

"Daddy, I'm firsty." Tyler stood in the doorway, an old stuffed bear under his arm, then hurried over to Billy Joe.

"How about a little milk?" Carlos asked.

Tyler nodded, and Carlos went to get it while Billy Joe took Tyler to the bathroom. When they returned, he gave Tyler the sippy cup, and he drank it down.

"Do you like inside camping?" Billy Joe asked as he led Tyler back into the other room. Carlos half expected Tyler to want his dad to sleep with him, but Tyler went right back down, judging by how quickly Billy Joe rejoined him. "He's already asleep again."

"Good." Carlos opened the other bedroom door and ushered Billy Joe inside.

Carlos loved his bedroom. The queen-size bed was perfect for him. The room was clean and plain, but not stark. Mrs. C had let him paint it, and he'd chosen a cool gray for the walls. The furniture Carlos had picked up at secondhand shops had been painted deep gray. The deep burgundy duvet matched the curtains, so there was color but not an overwhelming amount.

"You can use the bathroom first."

Carlos turned down the bed. After the ups and downs of the holiday, he wasn't sure what Billy Joe would be up for—probably just to sleep. They had planned this as a chance for them to be together, but the day had been... dammit, the holiday had turned into an emotional nightmare for Billy Joe. Carlos waited, sitting on the edge of the bed, until Billy Joe came out of the bathroom in his boxers.

Carlos waited for Billy Joe to climb between the sheets and then held him close. Comfort and care were what he needed now, and as much as Carlos might have wanted more, this was not the time.

Billy Joe rested his head on Carlos's shoulder, the two of them lying quietly together. Carlos turned out the lights and snuggled in close.

Silence settled around them.

Carlos's head spun with all that had happened, and he knew Billy Joe's had to be doing the same thing. He turned to Billy Joe and kissed him gently. "Just relax. It's behind us now. You did the right thing."

He felt Billy Joe nod, and then closed his eyes.

CARLOS STARTED awake as Billy Joe whined next to him in the darkness, waking him as well. He turned, meeting Billy Joe's piercing gaze. Carlos pulled him close, offering what comfort he could, thrilled at Billy Joe's presence in his bed.

"I'm tired of this. I'm tired of all of it. I need something good. I need something happy. I need…."

"I know. I do too." Carlos kissed Billy Joe slowly, gently. But Billy Joe had other ideas, pushing toward him, the heat of the kiss growing more intense.

Heat flowed through Carlos like liquid fire. Instantly he was hard and wanted to take Billy Joe in his arms, strip him of that last bit of cotton he'd been sleeping in, and lick his lean, whipcord body all over. He had to swallow to keep from drooling. Instead, he went to the bathroom, stripped down to his underwear, and turned out the light before returning to the bedroom.

Billy Joe lay on his back, legs and hips under the covers, arms behind his head. Carlos saw nothing other than Billy Joe's toned chest as it rose and fell with each breath. The man was hot. Carlos paused to take a breath and wait. Under normal circumstances, he would turn out the lights, get in bed, and be all over Billy Joe like white on rice. But he doubted that was what Billy Joe needed.

He glided slowly to the bed, pulled back the covers, and turned out the light. Then he turned to Billy Joe, sliding his hand over his belly, drawing him closer. "I know this doesn't…. I know yesterday was tough, and…." God, he hated it when he fumbled for words. "Look, I know we planned… well, to make love, but it's been a difficult day for you, and…."

Billy Joe pressed Carlos onto the mattress, pinning him there with his chest. "I appreciate that more than you know. Your friends were really nice, and you made a great dinner. It was… there was nothing you could do about the rest." Billy Joe kissed him. "I need this day to have some real happiness." He rested his head on Carlos's chest. "Make me forget the crap that can happen. I need you to show me that there is joy and wonder."

Carlos swallowed hard. "Is that what you really want?" He couldn't believe he was asking. If Billy Joe wanted joy, wonder, care, passion, and God knew what else, Carlos was more than ready to do his best to make that happen. Anticipation rose once again, but he tempered it with care and concern.

"Yes," Billy Joe answered breathily before kissing Carlos hard, lips demanding, his entire body shaking. "I need to forget about all of this."

"Are you sure that's a good idea?" Carlos asked and was tempted to bonk himself on the side of the head. Billy Joe wanted him. But he wasn't sure how he felt about being the guy Billy Joe used to forget his problems. He wanted to be more than that, and this had him a little confused.

Billy Joe nodded. "People drink whiskey and beer when they're upset, so they can forget. I'd much rather get drunk on you." He licked along Carlos's pec, and Carlos groaned softly.

"Dang…." Carlos whimpered when Billy Joe did it again, sucking lightly on a nipple. He closed his eyes, giving himself over to Billy Joe, who felt like a live wire. Energy and heat radiated off him to the point that Carlos just needed to let him take control.

When Billy Joe kissed him, the electricity between them shot to the ceiling, leaving him breathless and aching for more.

Billy Joe tugged at his lips, pulling on them before letting them slip away. He ran his hands down Carlos's sides, sliding his underwear away and off. Carlos opened his eyes just in time to watch as Billy Joe pivoted back and leaned a little forward, taking him in one swift movement that crossed his eyes. Carlos was about to yell at the top of his lungs, but jammed the heel of his hand between his lips instead. His head felt two sizes too big, the pressure mounting by the second as Billy Joe used his tongue in some swirling motion that drove him out of his mind.

"What are you doing to me?"

Billy Joe hummed around his cock, making Carlos grab the bedding, nearly tugging it loose from the mattress as he did his best to keep from flying off the bed. He writhed and shook as Billy Joe filled him with desire. His legs and feet tingled, hands going a little numb as the intensity grew and built. He'd never felt this way with anyone before. Yes, this was a blowjob and a damn good one, but it was so much more than that. Billy Joe was giving of himself, singlehandedly answering the question of whether there was a god…. Because Carlos was pretty sure he was about to see him any damn second.

Billy Joe pulled away just as Carlos reached the edge of his control. "Why'd you do that?" Carlos blinked, trying to see straight. He was covered in a thin film of sweat, breathing like a racehorse, and hot as hell.

"Because I want you," Billy Joe said, slipping off his boxers and reaching for the lube and a condom on the nightstand. Carlos was fine letting Billy Joe do the driving, so he was surprised when Billy Joe rolled the condom down Carlos's cock.

"Damn… you want me to…." Carlos's eyes widened as Billy Joe straddled him, lubed his fingers, and reached around behind. Carlos would give anything to see Billy Joe's fingers slipping inside himself. The thought made his cock jump, and damn it all, he was going to go off right now if he didn't get some control over his own damn body.

"Ready?" Billy Joe asked and angled back, his body opening around Carlos, sliding down him in a rush of heat and pressure, and he dang near lost it. Not only was the sensation mind-blowing, but Billy Joe was breathtaking, all lean and lanky, stretched out above him, his eyes half-lidded, mouth open, breathing deeply, his cock bouncing with each movement. Physically Carlos was in heaven; emotionally he fired on all cylinders and was quickly skating past heaven to bloody nirvana and beyond.

"That's it," Carlos breathed as Billy Joe huffed and rocked back and forth.

"To think we waited this long...." Billy Joe gasped, rolling his hips and driving Carlos out of his mind.

Carlos moaned and inhaled as deeply as he dared. "It's because we waited that it's so damn good." He thrust upward, tugging Billy Joe forward so he could kiss him. He needed to know this was more for Billy Joe than just the physical, because it sure as hell was for him. Billy Joe and Tyler had quickly come to mean so much to him. Carlos wanted Billy Joe in his life, not just now or for a few weeks, but long term. His mind raced in circles from the amazing physicality to the emotional attachment, and the way his chest warmed whenever Billy Joe looked at him with his deep, heated eyes. That look was for him and only for him. He could bask in that expression for the rest of his life if he were allowed.

"Billy Joe," Carlos whimpered. He stopped, hugging Billy Joe to him as he repositioned them on the bed. Carlos settled Billy Joe on his back and slid into him in one long stroke.

Air became a precious commodity as he leaned over him, their gazes locking instantly. They moved together, rocking in one symbiotic motion. Heaving breaths filled the room, echoing back to them. Carlos was never so grateful for a bedroom-door lock in his life. It wouldn't matter if the building fell down around them; his entire focus was in Billy Joe. Each breath and gasp told him what Billy needed, and Carlos responded, changing angle or speed until Billy Joe's eyes rolled to the back of his head and he quivered on the bedding. That was all Carlos wanted to see: Billy Joe in the throes of total ecstasy. Nothing could possibly be sexier or more fulfilling. His own pleasure was secondary; it was Billy Joe who came first in his mind.

"Gonna…," Billy Joe muttered between clenched teeth.

"Let it happen. Give yourself over and just let yourself be." Carlos drew out each sensation until Billy Joe tumbled into his release, with Carlos following right behind. He closed the slight distance between them to kiss Billy Joe gently.

"Carlos… I think I'm in love with you. You ain't got to say anything back, but there it is. You saved me, and I still wish I could figure out why, other than you're the nicest guy I've ever met in my life."

Carlos groaned. "Nice? You know that's the kiss of death. Nice," he teased.

"Then what?" Thankfully, Billy Joe was playing along.

Carlos pretended to think. "Hunky, hot, sexy, maybe amazing, stupendous?" He locked his gaze onto Billy Joe as his mirth slipped away. "Strong, caring, determined, an outstanding father, and someone I'd miss even if we'd never have met." Carlos swallowed hard and then kissed Billy Joe gently.

Now this, right here, was something to be thankful for.

Chapter 7

"I've told you how I'm willing to do this. So you figure it out or leave me alone," Carlos said from the kitchen the week after Thanksgiving, where he was likely talking to someone from his family... again.

Billy Joe figured he should just not have anything to do with them. Every time they called, it did nothing but upset Carlos, and Billy Joe hated the way they tried to bully him. He was also proud of the fact that Carlos stood up to them. It was an inspiration. Billy Joe wasn't so sure he'd be able to stand up to his own parents like that. Granted, if his family somehow found him, it was likely they'd come armed with more than words.

"That's enough, Luis. I'll contact an attorney and you can deal with him. I'm tired of being pressured and badgered like this. You all tossed me aside."

"Mr. Carlos is mad," Tyler said as he hurried to where Billy Joe sat on the sofa and crawled up onto his lap.

"He's not mad at you or me."

"That man who comed here?" Tyler asked, and Billy Joe nodded. "He's mean!" The wisdom of soon-to-be three-year-olds.

"Okay. That I'll agree to, but I don't want any more trouble, and you all need to leave me alone unless you can be nice." Carlos's tone gentled, and Billy Joe sighed. "You send me the papers with all that spelled out, and I'll sign them."

"Let's go make Carlos feel better," Billy Joe suggested.

Tyler got down off his lap and raced to his coloring book and crayons on the coffee table. "I color for him." He got to work, and Billy Joe went into the kitchen as Carlos set his phone aside.

"That's over." Carlos stood, hands on the counter, staring at the wall. "I thought...." His shoulders slumped forward. "It's totally stupid to be upset. But that's the last tie to my family... done and gone."

Billy Joe slid his arms around Carlos's waist, resting his head on the back of his shoulder blade, not saying anything. Words weren't going to help at a time like this. In his mind, Billy Joe always thought that things were similar with Carlos and his family and the way things were with Billy Joe's own. But that wasn't necessarily true. The difference was that Carlos held out hope. All these years, he'd hoped that his family would want him back, that they'd come to understand him, and that they'd realize they truly loved him and would welcome him back. That had to be why he took their calls. Granted, he was firm with them—hope only took things so far, and hurt governed the rest.

Billy Joe had no such illusions. He and Tyler had rocketed out of the bayou at the end of a potential gun. Billy Joe would do just about anything to stay the hell away from his family, and he'd abandoned hope long before he left.

"You understand, don't you?" Carlos turned, and Billy Joe nodded. "You just got here faster than I did."

Billy Joe shrugged. "I gave up hope for my family a long time ago." That had to be about the saddest thing he'd said in his life. Thankfully there had been no further contact with them since Thanksgiving, but whenever he thought about that phone call, a chill raced up his spine.

Carlos sighed and straightened. "I should have." His expression cleared, and he released a deep breath. "But I think it's over and I'll probably never hear from them again. The family is going to buy me out of the property, so that's the end of it."

"It sucks when your family isn't at all who they should be." Billy Joe could be the poster child for kids from dysfunctional families. "But what really stinks is that we can't do a damn thing about it, except try to move on and build a family of our own, hoping like hell we don't make the same mistakes." He tugged

Carlos closer, needing some of his strength, just as Carlos probably needed some of his. They could share it, and hopefully both of them would come out stronger.

"Tyler's birthday is in a few days. Maybe we should think about what we're going to do," Carlos offered. It was probably his way of changing the subject, but that was fine. Talking about their families was simply a lose-lose proposition any longer. "I was thinking we could take him to one of those activity centers. Get him a cake."

Billy Joe agreed with a smile. "I want him to have a real birthday, separate from Christmas. I think that's important. I got him a few things already and hid them under my bed," Billy Joe whispered.

"I'll get him some new books to read at bedtime, and maybe some new crayons and stuff," Carlos offered. "I know what he really wants, though."

"Me too. But he'll have to wait for a puppy. Maybe until he's a little older and I...." Billy Joe didn't want to say until they were more settled, but he wanted to feel more at home. It was hard for him to describe it.... Maybe less in flux before he got Tyler a pet? He was happy, for the most part. Billy Joe had a good job, and he was pleased with the state of his love life. He wished there was more alone time in it, though that couldn't really be helped. But it all seemed temporary. Billy Joe knew it could all be ripped away.

"You want to feel settled," Carlos supplied.

"Yeah." Billy Joe hugged Carlos, just holding him. "I want to be able to have a house with a yard where Tyler can play. I have some saved money in a CD, and I need to figure out how I can get it without alerting my father or any of his crony contacts."

Carlos nodded. "We've talked about that. We'll open an account at Bank of America and transfer the money there. Then once you get it, we can close that account and move it to the one you have at Citizens. We'll do that last one by cash so there isn't as much of an electronic trail that can be followed. No one is going to know where you took the cash, and they would have to have quite a few connections to follow the trail. We can start that tomorrow."

"Good." At least Billy Joe would have access to some more money and be in a little better position financially. He sighed. "I finished writing up everything I can remember about that night. It took me longer than I thought it would. I have the pages in my apartment. I included names of everyone and where they were. I was even able to draw a diagram of sorts of where everyone was. I don't know who I can give it to, but at least it isn't stuck in my head any longer. Maybe I can let it go." Billy Joe hugged Carlos once more, then backed away.

"Tyler, don't suck on the crayons. Okay, buddy?" Carlos said gently. Tyler had taken to sticking them in his mouth when he was drawing and wanted to think. Sometimes he'd end up with three or four of them in his mouth at once.

Tyler pulled them out and went back to his coloring.

"I think we need something to do. It's Saturday, and I don't want to go shopping because it will be nuts, but staying inside all afternoon isn't going to be good either." Billy Joe just needed to do something to take his mind off the worry nagging constantly in the back of his mind.

"Do you want to paint?" Carlos asked Tyler, who stood right up and jumped on his toes. "There's a paint-your-own-pottery place downtown. We could stop in there and see what they have. Tyler could make something fun, I bet." Carlos caught Tyler as he raced over and barreled into him. "I also saw that in January the library in town is having a children's reading hour Saturday mornings. We could sign Tyler up. It would be something the two of you could do together."

"That all sounds real good." Billy Joe wasn't so sure about the whole painting thing, but Tyler was excited about it, so he smiled and took him across the hall to get his coat. "We need to bundle up warm so we can go." Billy Joe got Tyler's coat on and his own as well before leaving the apartment.

The mailman was at the boxes in the lobby, so Billy Joe went on down, holding Tyler's hand, and opened his. There were a few bills inside and a supermarket flyer, as well as a typed envelope with no return address.

"Can you hold this for me?" Billy Joe asked, giving the mail to Tyler, who cradled it to his chest as though it were super important.

"Are you ready?" Carlos asked as he came down the stairs. Billy Joe held up the envelope, showing it to Carlos. "What is it?"

Billy Joe stared at the envelope and then carefully opened it. Inside was a single piece of folded paper. His legs shook as he unfolded it.

Did you really think I wouldn't find you?

Billy Joe dropped the page, his hand on the wall to steady himself.

"Jesus," Carlos sighed under his breath. "What kind of sicko is he?"

"Dad's all about control. He loves being a big man in the group."

Carlos held him, propping him up and steadying him at the same time.

"What do I do?" Billy Joe's first instinct was to pack up and get the hell out of town.

"Don't panic. He managed to look up an address, probably on the internet through one of those search services. However, he doesn't know that it's truly you, and he's still in Mississippi. What is he realistically going to do? Drive up here and try to haul you back? Remember, he has no power here."

Billy Joe took a deep, calming breath and shrugged. He turned to Tyler, who looked up at him with huge, wide eyes.

"Is that from Grampy?" Tyler picked up the paper and handed it back to him.

Billy Joe didn't want to touch it at all, but he did, placing it back in the envelope. "Yes. It is." Billy Joe took the mail and went upstairs, put it inside the apartment, and locked the door. He needed a chance to think clearly. "Let's go paint." This would all still be here when he got back. Carlos had promised Tyler some fun, and Billy Joe was going to make it happen, dammit.

"You going to be okay? We don't have to go anywhere if you don't want to. Either that or I can take Tyler and you can stay here, if that would help."

Carlos was so damn nice. Part of Billy Joe wanted to get the hell out of dodge, but he couldn't leave Carlos behind. In no time at all, he'd become so important to him that it was both exciting and frightening.

"Let's go. My father made my life miserable as hell for years. I'm not going to let that happen any longer."

"Way to go." Carlos lifted Tyler into his arms. "Let's go painting." He bounced Tyler, whose giggles echoed through the hallway. "Do you know what you want to make?"

"Hmmmm." Tyler put a finger to his lips. "A elephant."

Carlos tickled him, sending more giggles ringing brightly. How could anyone stay upset when hearing that sound?

"WOW," BILLY Joe sighed when they got back two hours and one Tyler-covered-in-paint later. "I don't think I've been in a place so loud in my life." There had been a birthday party with twenty six-year-olds there. Tyler had been in seventh heaven, talking to everyone as he painted two mugs—one for Daddy and one for Carlos.

Now Tyler was on Billy Joe's shoulder, having nearly fallen to sleep on the ride home. Billy Joe figured he'd feed him, get him in the bathtub, and Tyler would be out for the night. Billy Joe kissed Carlos goodbye and stumbled into the apartment with their bag of goodies. He set everything aside to finish drying and ran a bath, then got Tyler undressed and in the water.

Tyler loved bath time, but there was none of his usual joy. He let Billy Joe wash him, which was also unusual, and once he was dry and in his jammies, Billy Joe made him some supper and then Tyler went right to sleep without a second bedtime story.

By the time he was alone, sitting in front of the television, Billy Joe had a chance to think. A soft knock sounded as he was drifting off. Billy Joe got up and opened the door.

"I thought you could use something to eat. It's only some pasta and sauce, but I know how tired you are." Carlos set the pot on the table.

"Thanks." Billy Joe went to the table automatically and sat down while Carlos fussed and then joined him.

"You're a million miles away. It's the letter, isn't it?" Carlos dished up and placed a plate in front of him.

"Yes and no. I mean, it is the letter, and I've been doing a lot of thinking. My dad will push and push until he gets what he wants. It's what he does. Push and shove, push, push, push... and I have to keep Tyler safe. That's all that matters." Billy Joe picked up his fork. "I think there's only one way I can do that—make sure Dad goes to prison for his part in what happened to Hilliard." He sighed. "I don't have any other choice."

"Okay." Carlos chewed and looked at him partly like he was crazy and partly like he'd hung the moon.

"I think I'm going to have to call the FBI or something. I mean, I'm here and it took place in Mississippi, so I have to tell the Feds... or something. I really don't know." Billy Joe was starting to feel overwhelmed again, his leg bouncing under the table. "I have to make sure he can't touch us." Steel slowly slid up his backbone, and Billy Joe sat a little taller. "You were right."

"What about?" Carlos asked. "I need to know so I can make sure I do it again." He grinned, and Billy Joe chuckled, a touch of humor lightening the heavy mood.

119

"I owe this to Hilliard. He deserves justice, and I have to stop being scared of my own damned shadow all the time." Billy Joe took a deep breath and reached across the table to clutch Carlos's hand. "I'm so tired of it."

"You're doing the right thing. I can't know what this is like for you, but I'll be here. You have to know that." Carlos's expression shifted, and Billy Joe gasped as Carlos gazed at him. Warmth spread all through him, and Billy Joe realized for the first time, deep down, that he wasn't alone any longer. He'd been afraid of taking on his father and his past alone, but he didn't have to. He had Carlos.

"I'll make the phone call on Monday after we both get home from work." Billy Joe breathed deeply and held it, feeling better now that he'd decided on a course of action.

"I knew it," Carlos said softly. "I knew you had it in you."

Billy Joe rolled his eyes. "I suppose any dog can only be kicked so many times before it snaps."

Carlos shook his head. "No," he said firmly. "This isn't that at all. You're braver and stronger than that. You had the guts and the smarts to get yourself out. That takes fortitude and determination. You wanted a better life for Tyler, so you left everything you knew in the hope… just the hope… that you might find it. That isn't stupid, and it certainly isn't weak. So give yourself some credit and do what you think is right. Your dad doesn't have any power here."

"Don't be so sure. There are these types of groups in every state." Billy Joe knew that was true, but his father wasn't going to have his network of narrow-minded good old boys here.

"Maybe. But no one here is going to stick their neck out for him. Maybe they will in Mississippi, but my guess is that once you turn up the heat, his support is going to jump and run quickly as they can." Carlos smiled. "Stop worrying for now, eat your dinner, and then we'll relax on the sofa for a little while."

Dammit, Billy Joe felt like he could do just about anything as long as Carlos was there with him.

MONDAY CAME quickly enough, and a workday never passed so fast in all Billy Joe's life. Maybe that was what happened when something dreadful waited on the other end of it.

"Do you think I should go down to the office or something?" Billy Joe asked.

"Nope. I think you need to make a call. I looked up the number of the FBI field office in Jackson." Carlos set the paper in front of him on the table. They were at Carlos's, and Tyler hovered near him, knowing he was nervous. "Tyler and I are going to make him a tent in the other room and play camping for a while. Okay?" Carlos held out his hand, and Tyler went with him.

Billy Joe stared at the phone. He didn't pick it up until Tyler was out of the room, and even then he hesitated before unfolding the pages where he'd written down the details. This was frightening, and Billy Joe set down the phone again and raced to the bathroom. He got there just in time to lose what he'd had for lunch. He wiped his mouth with the back of his hand and jumped a little when Carlos slid his hand over his shoulder.

"You don't have to do this if—" Carlos whispered.

Billy Joe stood. "Yes, I do." This—all of it—had to come to an end, and this was the only way. Taking a deep breath, Billy Joe flushed the toilet and returned to the table. Carlos set a glass of orange juice in front of him. Billy Joe smiled nervously, and Carlos stroked his cheek, silent communication that said so much more than words ever could. Billy Joe drank a little of the juice to get the bile taste out of his mouth and picked up the phone.

Carlos, returning to the bedroom where he and Tyler were playing camping, stopped at the door to turn around. Billy Joe caught his gaze and held his breath, dialing the numbers from the paper. Carlos went inside as the call was answered.

"FBI field office, Jackson," a woman said.

"Yes. I need to report a murder," Billy Joe said in as level a voice as possible. "I witnessed it on October twenty-seventh."

"Yes, sir." There was a slight hesitation. "Let me...." She hesitated once more, and then the phone clicked and a man came on the line.

"This is Special Agent Carter. May I help you?" The voice held no hint of a southern accent, which made Billy Joe feel better. If the special agent wasn't local, then he wasn't going to have any ties to Jackson.

Billy Joe took a breath and then began again. "I witnessed the murder of Hilliard Gustafson on October twenty-seventh of this year by a white supremacy group in the woods outside Jackson."

"Please hold on a minute," Agent Carter said, and Billy Joe heard clicking. "A missing persons report has been filed. But... are you saying he's dead?"

"Yes. My name is William Joseph Massier, and I witnessed the murder. I can provide you with the place, dates, names of a lot of the people in attendance, as well as the name of the person who shot him in the head." Billy Joe closed his eyes. He didn't want to relive all that again, but he had to do it. Hilliard deserved justice. "It was at a rally out in Culver's Woods. I didn't see what they did with the body. I wasn't supposed to be there...."

"Massier.... Massier...."

"Yes. My father was the man leading the rally," Billy Joe clarified. "He didn't actually kill Hilliard, but it happened in front of him and he allowed and encouraged it." Billy Joe's nerves spiked again.

A soft squeak caught his attention and Billy Joe turned. Carlos peered out of the bedroom door, smiling slightly. Billy Joe knew he was concerned and returned the smile.

"All right, why don't you tell me everything that happened? And I'm going to record this call so I can get the details. Let's start with your name and where you live."

Billy Joe hesitated but figured if he was going to do this, he would need to do it all the way. He gave his name, address, phone number, and explained why he was in Pennsylvania and how he'd gotten there. "I think it was my dad who had called the rally. He and his cronies were upset about something. Who knows what? They were being secretive, but I've been to enough of these things and decided to follow him." Billy Joe explained where he'd been and his horror at seeing someone he knew. "I was paralyzed, afraid and sick because I couldn't save him." He cleared his throat. "I nearly wet myself, I was so scared." He pulled open the piece of paper and listed all the names he could remember being there, as well as the name of the person who'd pulled the trigger.

"How do you know all these details?" Special Agent Carter asked.

"Because I grew up around all these people. The group was as big a part of my life as going to church. I've been around them my entire life. But I was never one of them. See, I knew Hilliard... he and I were friends." The tears welled up and he couldn't stop them.

"Why did they kill him?" Carter asked.

Billy Joe wiped his eyes and turned as Tyler raced across the room, climbed up on his lap, and held him. Billy Joe put his free arm around him, holding Tyler as Carlos placed his hands on his shoulders. "Hilliard was gay. He saved my life and helped me realize who I was. I saw this and realized that I was next." Billy Joe put his hand over Tyler's ear as he spoke. "See, I'm gay. My dad would probably kill me too if he could. So I got the heck out of town and the state." He leaned his head back against Carlos.

"Does anyone know you witnessed this incident?"

Billy Joe chuckled. "No. I didn't make some kind of announcement. I left and took my son with me. He deserves a better childhood than I had growing up with those types of people." He saw now how that colored almost everything he could remember.

"All right." Billy Joe could almost see him writing furiously on the other end of the phone. "Why did you wait so long to come forward?"

Billy Joe thought a little while. "At first I was scared and needed to get away. I thought I'd be safe if I was gone. I did call the tip line from Memphis, but I couldn't get my thoughts together and they asked me if I was drunk…. Then I thought about it. Hilliard was my friend and he helped me and deserves justice. So in the end, that's why I called you. But I will do anything to keep my son safe and away from him. I don't want my father to influence my son's life. This family legacy of hate has got to end somewhere." Billy Joe took a deep breath and released it, his insides finally settling down. "And before you ask, I will not come back to Mississippi. If you all want to talk to me, you can come here and I will meet with you, sign statements, and you can ask me more questions. But I am not returning to Mississippi." He felt better making that statement.

"Hopefully you won't have to," Agent Carter said. Billy Joe noticed he didn't make any promises, and that was probably all he could hope for.

"You don't understand. I think my father might have found out my address. He sent me a letter, a veiled threat. But he might be fishing for a response of some sort." Billy Joe sighed. "I want to be safe, and I think now that the only way that is going to happen is if you put him in jail." There. He'd said it. He took a deep breath. "What else can I tell you?" Billy Joe needed to get this over with.

He answered questions to provide details as to where the rally was and how he knew Hilliard, and then questions about where the various people were. Carlos took a photo of his diagram and emailed it to Agent Carter. He even sent copies of what he'd written down. If Billy Joe was going to do this, he had to do it all the way.

"One final question. Had you seen anything like this before?" Special Agent Carter asked.

"You mean, like a murder?" Billy Joe asked quietly. "No. But I was with my dad when I was ten years old and he and his friends lit a cross on the yard of one of the little boys in school." He glanced up at Carlos as he turned away, then took Tyler off his lap and carried him back to the camping room. Billy Joe continued. "It was supposed to toughen me up." He suddenly felt so damn alone, wringing his hands. "I used to go to rallies. Heck, they were like family picnics, with confederate flags, swastikas, and talk about how the white man was going to rise up and take this country back." It was a lot worse than that, but he didn't need to talk about it. Agent Carter probably got the idea. "I never saw nobody killed before."

"Are you aware of any other illegal activities?"

Billy Joe thought and shook his head before realizing he wasn't answering. "I don't think so, but you don't start with murder, do you? I bet if you start digging, you'll find a whole mess of stinking filth."

"Okay. Is this a good number to get in touch with you? I'm going to write all this up and will look into it. And you're sure you don't have any idea where the body is?"

"No. I didn't stick around to hear anything more about it. But if I were to guess, I'd say the first alligator swamp they came across. Dump it in and the gators make quick work of it." Billy Joe wiped his eyes again. "Hilliard deserved so much fucking better than this."

"Well, thank you for coming forward. I will be in touch."

Billy Joe hung up the phone and put his head down on the table, letting the tears come. His entire life up until a few weeks ago had been washed away, burning in a fire of his own making, and now all he had left was Tyler and the ashes of everything else. There was no going back. All his bridges had been burned. He had to move forward.

For the last six weeks, ever since he'd seen Hilliard's murder, he'd been living in abject fear. Billy Joe took a deep breath and tried to think. His life had become a tightrope, and it felt like he was walking over a sea of flames.

"Billy Joe," Carlos said, winding his arms around him, holding him so tight that he could hardly breathe, but it was exactly what he needed. "It's okay. I'm here."

"Where's Tyler?" Billy Joe needed to see and hold him.

"In the bedroom playing hide and seek. I need to go find him in a second, but I wanted to make sure you were all right."

Billy Joe sniffed. "You aren't disappointed in me?" He wiped his eyes yet again.

"What for? The stuff you said about growing up? That wasn't you. I didn't think you wanted Tyler to hear it, that's all. If I could, I would have stayed with you the entire time." Carlos lifted his head off the table and kissed him. "I'm so proud of you." He wiped the back of his hand across Billy Joe's eyes. "I think I was just witness to the bravest thing I've ever seen in my life." Carlos kissed him again, this time harder.

Tyler's voice drifted out of the other room, followed by giggles. "Uncle Carlos, you have to find me."

Billy Joe raised his eyebrows and Carlos shrugged.

"He asked what he should call me. Is that okay?"

"I like it." Billy Joe really did. Carlos was family, and unlike his blood family, he could rely on him. "He cares about you so much. Sometimes when we're home alone, he asks where you are and if you can come over to play with him." Billy Joe smiled. "You better go find him."

"Are you going to be okay?" Carlos asked.

"Yes. The ball has started rolling now, and I don't think there's anything I can do to stop it any longer. My father can try what he wants now, but he and his friends have gone too far. And somehow I doubt the FBI is going to let any of them off the hook. Even in these strange political times, murder isn't going to be condoned."

Carlos nodded and hurried away toward the bedroom, calling out to Tyler that he was going to get him. Of course, Tyler giggled the entire time as he tried to hide. Billy Joe followed to the bedroom door, watching as Carlos played along to laughter before finally "finding" Tyler under the desk.

"Are you hungry?" Carlos asked as he lifted Tyler toward the ceiling to a chorus of additional giggles. "What do you want for dinner?"

"Chicken nuggets," Tyler yelled, bouncing as soon as Carlos set him on his feet. "Donald's."

"Okay. How about I go out and get the food so we can eat here?"

Billy Joe nodded. "I appreciate that." He didn't want to go anywhere right now. He was wrung out completely. "You and I can watch television for a while." Billy Joe sighed, and Carlos leaned in to kiss him gently.

"I won't be gone long. I know what he wants."

Billy Joe gave Carlos his order and sat on the sofa with Tyler, letting him watch television.

TYLER WAS a barrel of energy all through dinner and well into the evening. Bath time and stories didn't calm him down much. Billy Joe got him settled in his "tent," but he lay awake, asking for story after story. Billy Joe's patience ran so thin and he was so tired, he barely held back the urge to sit down and cry. Finally Tyler lay down, and Billy Joe left him in the room, closing the door.

"Is he asleep?"

Billy Joe shook his head. "No. I hope he will be soon, but he was just lying there, singing softly to himself when I left. Sometimes I just have to leave him alone so he can go to sleep on his own," he whispered, settling next to Carlos and leaning on his shoulder. "How can you stay through all this crap? I wouldn't blame you if you ran screaming from our lives and didn't want to have anything to do with us. I just know there's going to be a shit-ton of crap coming my way because of this."

"I've waded through a ton of shit before, and I'll do it again. It isn't important." Carlos took his hand. "At least not as important as you and Tyler." He grinned wickedly. "Someone has to look after you."

"Really?" Billy Joe cocked his eyebrows. "Is that so?"

Carlos nodded. "I'll have your back just like you have mine. That's the way these things work. And if your father or anyone comes up here to try to cause trouble, they'll learn that things are done very differently here than they are in Mississippi. There's no love for their kind here. Last year a group tried to rally in Harrisburg, and enough counterprotestors showed up to block them from actually reaching their site. The rally ended up with a dozen people looking stupidly at each other, surrounded by picketers. They didn't know whether to shit or go blind."

"So what do we do?"

"We're going to call the police and report the letter your father sent you. Give them a copy of everything we sent to the FBI so they know what's going on. Their support is going to be needed if anyone shows up here."

Billy Joe shrugged. "Do you really think they have the time to watch over me and Tyler? If they're like the police anywhere, they're overwhelmed and short-staffed. Yes, we can call them and see what they'll do, but it's likely what we give them will sit in a file until something happens." He didn't mean to shit on Carlos's idea, but….

"You have a letter—"

"With no return address. It's just my word that it's from him because I recognize his handwriting. There isn't anything overtly threatening in it. That's the problem. Yeah, I can explain what I saw and that I've contacted the FBI. Maybe that will get their attention." Billy Joe closed his eyes. "I'm feeling too much like

128

I've been run over by a truck to deal with this anymore. The whole thing is wearing me out."

"Then let's go to bed. You're tired...."

"How about a movie or something quiet?"

Carlos used the remote and found the miniseries *The Pillars of the Earth*. He started the first episode and turned out the lights. Billy Joe curled up on the sofa, and Carlos lay in front of him. Billy Joe held him, his head on a pillow. He got caught up in the story, holding Carlos and doing his best to relax a little. Eventually he closed his eyes as the cathedral went up in flames. He listened to the show, soaking in some of Carlos's heat and closeness until the program ended and Carlos sat up. The warmth slipping away did more to rouse him than anything else. If Carlos had stayed where he was, Billy Joe probably would have fallen to sleep and stayed that way the entire night.

"Come to bed." Carlos tugged him to his feet, led him to the bed, and ten minutes later, Carlos lay pressed to him once more.

CHAPTER 8

"CARLOS," ANGIE said from behind him. "What's going on with you?" She glared at him as he stared into the blank library display case. "That isn't going to fill itself, you know. Are you waiting for some sort of inspiration?"

He shook his head. "No. It's…." Carlos pulled the cart closer and started building the display he'd put together of books that had been banned for various reasons. It was becoming important that students understand what censorship truly meant. He did this kind of display every few years, with a new batch of students. It seemed to be a perpetual lesson. Carlos looked around to verify that they were pretty much alone. "Billy Joe. He got another letter from his father." He was beginning to wonder how hard it was to put together a case against the bastard and stick his ass in jail.

"Is he holding it together?" Angie asked.

"As best he can. Last night he shook when he got that second note. It was definitely a threat, even if it was as vague as the first one. He called the police and explained the entire situation, but he was right. There's only so much they can do. I want him to be safe."

"His father is at the other end of the country. Does he think he's going to drive or fly up to get to him?" Angie asked.

Carlos sighed, nodding slowly. "I think he's been terrorized by them so much, he doesn't know what to expect. In the evenings he stays at either my place or his. He doesn't want to go out, and all the curtains are pulled closed. Tyler's birthday is tonight and we're taking him to the Fun Emporium. They have an indoor bouncy castle, go-carts, laser tag, and a bunch of games. We wanted to do something fun for him, but I'm afraid Billy Joe is going to spend the evening on high alert or something." He scratched his head.

"That sounds like fun."

"Then come. I think other people might help him relax. I don't know. We have a cake for Tyler, and presents. It's getting close to Christmas, but we want him to be able to celebrate his birthday separate from that."

Angie chuckled. "Andy loves that sort of thing. He grew up with video games and always kills it at the arcade."

"Why don't we meet at our place at five thirty and we can go over from there? They have pizza and stuff, but I was thinking we could eat somewhere first and then go there for cake and games." Carlos forced a smile.

"Sounds good." She patted his shoulder gently. "Things are going to work out. We worry about stuff all the time that doesn't ever happen."

Carlos thanked her and turned to his task. If Billy Joe's father showed up, they'd call the police. What worried Carlos was how Billy Joe was letting his family have so much influence over him, even from a distance.

Like he was one to talk. At least the business with his family was nearly concluded, and like it or not, for good or bad, he was almost done with them forever.

"Sometimes I wonder how much we can take," he said softly, placing a book in the case and then another.

Angie rested her hand on his shoulder. "Are you worried about what he can take, or how much you can?" Sometimes she was too damned insightful for words. "It's okay to admit that you're a little overwhelmed. Anyone would be."

Carlos set the book he was holding down and turned back to her. "I have to be strong for Billy Joe and Tyler. They need me."

She nodded. "But you need them too." She grinned. "Despite the troubles you two seem to have and the battles you're fighting, you smile so much more than you did before you met him, and there's a light in your eyes when you talk about him. It's the same one I see in Andy's eyes sometimes and know that

131

he loves me. And that no matter how bad things might get, he'll be there to help me slay the dragons." She picked up a copy of *The Hobbit*, holding it in front of him. "No matter what comes—the good, the bad, and the ugly—it's better with someone you love." She patted his shoulder and drew her hand away. "You know what I think?"

Carlos shrugged. "That you're a nosy busybody sometimes?"

"Duh." Angie grinned, taking the teasing the way Carlos knew she would. "But I'm going to give you the benefit of my brilliance anyway." She flipped her hair back, and Carlos rolled his eyes. "Seriously, love that comes out of picnics and rainbows, lollipops and sunshine, that's the easy kind of love, and often it withers and dies when the shit hits the fan. But the love that grows out of hardship and shared adversity is strong and deep. It has to be in order to take root at all."

He sighed. "So you're saying it's a good thing all this shit is happening?" He refused to believe that.

"No. What I'm saying is that if you can fall in love through all this, then it's strong and the real thing. It's the kind you can depend on." She nodded to stress her point. "Are you going to walk away from Billy Joe when things get hard? If his family shows up? Or are you going to fight them as hard as he does?" She nodded, turned, and walked back toward the desk.

Carlos stared after her and then turned back to the display. She sure as heck knew how to make an exit. And in a strange way, Carlos felt better. He returned to his work, trying to put the display together in an interesting way, but it was just a case of books with a sign.

"It's dull," Marie said as she passed. "What if you got maintenance to change out the bulbs in the case for red ones? That will make the display more ominous and catch their attention."

"Awesome idea." Carlos pulled out his phone and sent a note down to maintenance with his request, then finished setting up the display after noting that there was room for them to change the bulbs, provided they had any that would work.

"THE ARRANGEMENT looks good, and these are books many of our students will know," Marie said as Carlos stepped back to take a look. "I get so sick of fighting the same battles year after year sometimes." She smiled. "You have a minute?" she asked, and Carlos finished packing up his supplies and pushed the cart back to their offices. Marie's was next to his, and she went inside and returned with a wrapped gift. "This is for Tyler."

"Marie, that's so sweet of you." He smiled and hugged her gently. "It was so nice of you to remember. We're taking him out tonight."

"I heard. Make sure the little guy has a great night, okay?" Where they were going was definitely not a Marie kind of place. She turned toward the clock, and Carlos followed her gaze. "You'd better get things wrapped up or you're going to be late, and you don't want to keep that little dose of sunshine waiting."

"No, I don't." Carlos got caught up on his email and met one of the maintenance guys as he was leaving. "Hey, Michael." He showed him the case and explained what he wanted to do. "Just leave the regular bulbs in my office so we can replace them when we change the display. It will save you a trip."

"Will do," Michael said. "You need to get home. Billy Joe already left to pick up Tyler."

"Thanks." Carlos hurried out to his car and was off home.

Tyler met him at the door with a conical purple birthday hat on, grinning from ear to ear.

"They had a party for him at day care," Billy Joe explained. "He insisted on wearing his birthday hat."

"It looks very festive." Carlos set down his bag and lifted Tyler into the air. "Happy birthday."

Tyler giggled. "I'm big. I'm three." He squealed as Carlos held him way up high, then set him on his feet and tickled him lightly. The joy that rang through the hall was glorious.

"Yes, you are." He knelt down to talk directly to Tyler. "I need to go clean up a little, and then you and your daddy and me are going to have some dinner and then go to the play place. Okay?"

Tyler nodded with a grin.

Carlos stood again. "Angie and Andy are going to be here soon. Andy apparently is a huge kid. I hope that's okay."

"Of course." Billy Joe took Tyler's hand, and they headed back toward the apartments.

"I'll call and verify arrangements. Give me fifteen minutes and we can go." Carlos went inside, got the presents together in a bag, and raced to the bathroom. He cleaned up quickly, changed clothes, and went across the hall to knock on Billy Joe's door.

Billy Joe opened it, talking on the phone. "I see." He smiled nervously. "Well, that's very good. He can't leave the city?" He listened again and his smile grew. The tension Billy Joe had carried in his shoulders and torso seemed to leach away. "Do they know it was me?" He turned to Carlos. "It's the FBI," he said softly.

Carlos went inside and joined Tyler on the sofa, where he was waiting, feet rocking back and forth. "He isn't going to be very long."

Tyler nodded, looking serious. "He means Grampy. Daddy's mad at him." He looked seconds from tears.

Carlos gathered him in a hug. "Sometimes grown-ups have to deal with things that aren't very nice. You don't have to worry about anything, though. Your daddy isn't mad at you, and he loves you very much." Carlos let Tyler climb on his lap, rocking slowly until Billy Joe hung up.

"Everything is all right now." Billy Joe smiled, really smiled, with genuine warmth, for the first time in a while. "It's going to be fine from now on." He lifted Tyler into his arms as he spun around the room. "Everything is going to be great." Billy Joe held Tyler up until he almost touched the ceiling, flying him around the room. "Let's go get you something eat." Billy Joe looked at Carlos. "The p-r-e-s-e-n-t-s are in the bedroom. Can you get the bag and put it in the car while I get Tyler's coat on?"

Carlos easily found the bag, and while Tyler was occupied, he made it out of the apartment and down to the car. Angie and Andy pulled in as Billy Joe and Tyler joined him, and once Tyler was in his seat, they all headed for McDonald's. It wasn't their favorite place, but Tyler loved it and it was his birthday. Andy played Happy Meal cars with Tyler, running them around the table. Tyler was thrilled, and it gave everyone else a chance to finish eating. Once they were done, they headed to the Fun Emporium.

"I called and reserved a room under the name Miras," Carlos told the girl behind the desk when they entered. "It's for a birthday party." He had the cake balanced on one hand and a small bag of presents in the other. Billy Joe held Tyler by the hand, with more presents on the other. It looked like they were moving in.

"Hey!" Angie said as she approached and relieved Carlos of the cake box. "Are you excited for your birthday party?" she asked Tyler, who could barely stand still, he was so excited, driven even more so by all the flashing lights, game music, and screams of delight from everywhere.

"Yes. I have it." The desk girl pointed. "Just down the hall, room four."

Carlos thanked her and led the way to a brightly painted room with tables and chairs in primary colors. Tyler raced to one of the tables and climbed into his seat, looking expectantly over the table. "I'm ready."

"I know you are." Carlos set the plates and forks that he'd packed on the table while Angie put out the cake.

"Hi, Mr. Miras, Mrs. Hofstadter," Heidi said as she came in the room. "You must be the birthday boy." She grinned at Tyler. "I like your hat."

"Hi, Heidi. How are you doing?" Carlos had worked with Heidi on one of her junior papers late last year. She was a gifted student. "This is Tyler and his dad, Billy Joe, and Angie's husband, Andy."

Heidi waved at them. "Can I bring you anything?" She took out a pad.

"Pizza," Tyler said, bouncing. "Pepperponies." Sometimes he was a bottomless pit. Carlos ordered a pizza, and everyone got drinks.

"I'll be right back."

Carlos started laying the presents out on the table. Tyler's eyes widened when he saw all the gifts. He and Billy Joe probably had gone a little overboard, but the look on Tyler's face was worth it.

"Are those for me?"

"Yes." Angie added another to the stack.

"Wow." It was like he wasn't sure where to start. Billy Joe handed him a present, and Tyler ripped off the paper. "Oh, I love it," he exclaimed as he held up the box of Legos. "Thank you." He smiled at Angie. Then he opened another present. "Oh, I love it." Over and over again, with each gift, he repeated the same phrase and thanked the person who gave it to him. All four of them did their very best to keep from laughing as the gifts piled up. The biggest one for last.

"What is it?" Billy Joe asked.

"Something I saw and thought was perfect," Carlos whispered.

Tyler nearly sent everything tumbling to the floor as he pulled off the wrapping, gasping when he saw the picture on the box.

"This way you can play camping with your very own tent."

Tyler slipped off the seat and did a little butt-wiggling happy dance.

Heidi came in and nearly dropped the pizza when she saw it. "Hey, buddy, here's your pizza." She placed it on the table with plates and silverware.

Tyler raced over, hyped up on presents. It was an amazing sight, seeing the little guy happy like that. Billy Joe sat next to him and took Carlos's hand under the table. Tyler was excited and all smiles. They dished up the pizza, each taking a slice.

"Can I play?" Tyler picked up the tent box, hugging it to himself as he waddled over.

"Why don't you wait until you get home? Uncle Carlos can help you set it up." Billy Joe helped Tyler get settled. "Eat your pizza first, and then we'll go out and play some games."

"Have you heard anything more about your family?" Angie asked Billy Joe quietly.

Billy Joe nodded, turning to Angie and Carlos. "I got a call just before we left. The FBI investigated and found plenty of evidence. They apparently were able to get people to turn on each other." He smiled, and Carlos squeezed his fingers under the table. He figured Billy Joe had gotten some good news. "My dad is being held for conspiracy to commit murder, as are a bunch of other men. The killer is in jail without bail, but someone posted bail for my dad. The judge ordered him on twenty-four-hour surveillance, though, so he's got an ankle-cuff thing. He can't leave Mississippi and is basically confined to the house."

"That's great!" Carlos said softly, bumping Billy Joe's shoulder. It was about time they got some good news on that front.

"It gets better. They didn't have to reveal where they got their tip, so they don't know that I was the one who turned them all in. Special Agent Carter said that when they got to the scene of the incident, there was still enough evidence lying around to put things together pretty well." Billy Joe sniffed slightly. "They haven't found Hilliard, though."

Carlos put an arm around his shoulder. "They will. It's a matter of time, and then at least his family can have some closure."

Billy Joe wiped his nose. "I'm worried about my mom, though. This is going to be really hard on her." Though she and his father probably deserved whatever happened. He sighed softly. "I know she condoned a lot of my father's behavior over the years, so I guess she's paying for that." He really needed to stop this and remember that he'd left both of his parents because of the atmosphere they helped contribute to and the things they allowed to happen. "You reap what you sow."

Carlos nodded. "Does it sound like your dad is going to try to fight the charges?"

"I don't know. I wasn't told, and I suppose he has to figure that out. If he does, then I'll probably have to go testify. I'm hoping there's enough other evidence that I don't have to go. But if that's what it takes, then I'll do it." Billy Joe finished his pizza.

Carlos ate about half of his and pushed the rest aside. It wasn't all that good anyway. "Are you ready for games?" he asked Tyler, who jumped off his chair.

"I am," Andy said.

"I'll stay here where it's quiet. You boys go have fun." Angie sat back, and Carlos took Tyler's hand.

"Then let's go." He led the way out, got a card, and put some money on it. "How about Skee-Ball?" He helped Tyler get set up and showed him how to play. Tyler threw the balls down and got a few tickets. Billy Joe did pretty well on the machine next to them and ended up with a whole bunch of tickets when he nearly maxed out his game.

"Again!"

Carlos set them all up with another game, and Tyler had a blast. He didn't do any better, but he had fun, and that was all that mattered. Tyler jumped up and down, doing his butt-wiggle happy dance each time he got a ticket.

CARLOS UNLOCKED the door, and Billy Joe carried a sleepy Tyler inside.

"Camping, Daddy," Tyler whined, struggling to get down as soon as they were inside.

"I'll go get the rest of the stuff from the car," Carlos offered, and hurried back out to get the bags of gifts from the back. When he returned, Tyler was crying and pushing Billy Joe away. Then Tyler raced across the hall to Carlos's door, which was still locked.

"Camping, Uncle Carlos," Tyler said, turning to him, tears streaking his cheeks as he pushed out his lower lip. Man, he had that "I'm so sad" look down pat.

"You need to come in and get ready for bed," Billy Joe said.

Tyler ran to the bag of gifts, hauled out the tent, and dragged it inside. "Camping sleep." He set the box down and did his best to try to open it. "I camping sleep."

"I'll help you put up your tent if you listen to your daddy, okay?" Carlos set the bag of presents off to the side and knelt down, and Tyler went right into his arms. "It's your birthday. You don't need to act like that."

"Birthday camping," Tyler countered, and there was little Carlos could say about that. He lifted his gaze as Billy Joe put his hand over his mouth.

"Do you mind?" Billy Joe asked, and Carlos shook his head. "Come on with me. Uncle Carlos will set your tent up in the living room and you can sleep there."

"Camping room." Tyler pointed across the hall and raced out the door, which Carlos had thought he'd closed. Billy Joe went after him, and Carlos picked up the long box and opened it.

Billy Joe brought Tyler back inside, closing the door.

"It's fine," Carlos said, suddenly feeling selfish. If Tyler slept in the extra room in his place, then Billy Joe could stay with him… and that sent a thrill racing through him. "I'll go set up the tent and sleeping bag while you get him bathed and ready for bed." He carried the box across the hall and unlocked his door. Carlos took off his coat and then opened the box, pulling out the pieces of the light vinyl play tent.

Setting it up took longer than he expected. But by the time everything was together and the sleeping bag spread out on the floor, Tyler raced in wearing his teddy bear pajamas with feet.

"I love it," he exclaimed as soon as he saw the red-and-blue tent, and crawled inside, scrambling into the sleeping bag.

Billy Joe read Tyler a story while Carlos made some tea and waited on the sofa. When Billy Joe joined him, he looked just as tired but had a smile on his lips.

Carlos handed him a mug. "It's hot, so be careful."

Billy Joe took a sip, set the mug on the table, and leaned close. Energy zinged between them as the kiss instantly grew heated.

Carlos tugged Billy Joe to him. "It's good to see you happy and relaxed. There was always something weighing you down, but that seems gone now." He pressed Billy Joe down on the cushions.

"I know. My dad can't go anywhere, and he and his friends are being investigated or in jail already. There's going to be enough trouble for them that they aren't going to have a chance to worry about me anymore." Billy Joe grinned wide. "I'm free of them."

Carlos chuckled and nodded. "I know you feel that way, but I think you were free of them as soon as you decided to get out of there." He climbed off the sofa, taking Billy Joe's hand. "Come on. We've both had a long day."

"It's still early." Billy Joe sat up and got to his feet.

"Yeah." Carlos was counting on that.

They checked on Tyler, who was sound asleep, lying on his side. They shared a smile and then left the room, closing the bedroom door behind them.

Carlos hugged Billy Joe tightly, their kisses fast, deep, bodies shaking as Carlos pulled away only long enough to tug Billy Joe's polo over his head. Damn, he was beautiful. Carlos stepped back just to admire him for a few seconds. Billy Joe crossed his arms over his chest, and Carlos gently soothed them back to his side. "Don't be self-conscious."

"But you're looking at me like—"

"A man who loves you," Carlos finished.

Billy Joe shook his head. "How can you? After all the crap I've brought with me. How...?"

"What crap? So you have a crappy family. So do I. Do you really think that matters?" Carlos placed his hand in the center of Billy Joe's chest. "I never thought I'd have a family of my own. I didn't think it was possible. In a few weeks, you and Tyler have come to feel like the family I always wanted but never thought could be mine. You did that. And it wasn't because of your family or what you have... or anything like that. It's because you're you." He slid a hand around the back of Billy Joe's neck and tugged him into a kiss. "I fell in love with you."

Billy Joe nodded and put his arms around Carlos's neck. "I can hardly believe it. I thought... well... I.... It's hard for me to believe that someone could love me. Lord knows my mom and dad thought I was useless until I had Tyler and made them grandparents."

"You aren't useless—you never were."

"I know that now. Thanks to you." Billy Joe guided Carlos closer. "I know a lot of things now." Billy Joe kissed him, sending a pulse of heat racing all through him from head to toe. "I love you, Carlos. I do... at least I think so." He stroked Carlos's cheeks, sending a thrill running up his spine.

"Do you want to explain that or leave me to guess?" Carlos asked, confused by the difference between Billy Joe's words and the intensity burning in his eyes. Maybe what Billy Joe felt was just lust, and while it was nice being lusted over, it wasn't what he'd hoped for.

"I grew up in a house ruled by hate. Every day of my life, I heard my parents spout this line about who wasn't as good as they were."

Carlos nodded. He understood now. He was still one of those inferior people. He tensed and pulled away. "I see." All these weeks, Carlos had thought Billy Joe really cared, but it was just some act or him seeing only what he wanted to see.

Billy Joe shook his head. "I don't think so. In my house growing up, I was raised to hate. That was what I knew, and it was all I knew. My dad wasn't loving, and I spent most of my life trying to avoid his wrath and not to make him mad at me. But I think my father is angry with the entire world. I've been reading, and I know for some people in the group, it's a path to power and a leg up in politics. For others it's safety, I guess. They are better off in a group than they are alone. I can see and understand that. Doesn't make it right, though. My dad is all about the hate. He thinks he's entitled to shit from everyone and isn't willing to work for it. Not really."

Carlos waited, hoping Billy Joe would explain what he meant, because right now, Carlos was at a loss and feeling exposed and emotionally naked. He'd told Billy Joe that he loved him and…. His thoughts faltered.

"I grew up with hate. Not love. I didn't know what that truly was until I had Tyler. I know he loves me, and I adore him with everything I have. I don't even know what a good marriage looks like because, God knows, my parents' is as dysfunctional as anything else in our family." Billy Joe took his hands. "I'm saying that I love you… if I know what love is. I don't have anything to use as a basis. I know I'd hurt myself before I'd hurt you and that I want to be here with you more than just about anything." He tugged Carlos closer. "I want to go to bed with you, and not just for sex. I want to sleep with you, wake up with you, and I want you to help me raise Tyler." Billy Joe paused and wrapped him in a hug. "I guess maybe that's the definition of real love. My parents were selfish—still are. But I don't want to be selfish with you. I want to share the most important thing in my life with you: my son." Billy Joe squeezed him even tighter.

Carlos didn't have a clue what to say. Suddenly, him saying that he loved Billy Joe seemed inadequate. "How am I supposed to compete with that?"

Billy Joe chuckled. "This isn't a competition." He clutched Carlos, and Carlos loved the heat as it washed over him. Before Carlos could react, Billy Joe turned them, pressing him back against the bed. His legs hit the mattress and he tumbled backward, laughing as he bounced. Billy Joe stood over him, shirtless, smiling as brightly as the morning sun. He wore happiness well, and Carlos was pleased to bask in it for a little while.

"I guess not." Carlos struggled to get up, but Billy Joe pushed him down, pulling at his shirt until Carlos got it off. It ended up on the floor, along with his shoes. He desperately wanted out of his pants, which had grown way too tight. Billy Joe leaned over him, and Carlos wound his arms around his neck, tugging him down until their lips met. God, that was heady. Billy Joe tasted of mint and herbs; underneath, his maleness, rich and deep, came through, sending Carlos's mind in a whirl.

"I love you, Carlos," Billy Joe whispered, deepening the kiss.

Carlos held him closer, wriggling his hips against Billy Joe's, needing more sensation, closeness... everything. His legs shook as Billy Joe slid downward to capture a nipple between his hot lips while lightly pinching the other until Carlos had difficulty catching his breath. He whimpered softly, clenching his eyes closed because he could only deal with so much at once. He wanted more, and when he got it, the sensation nearly overwhelmed, sending wave after wave of heated pleasure racing through him.

"Billy Joe," he groaned, holding him for dear life.

The thing was, he was still mostly dressed and was already reaching the edges of desire. Thankfully, for his control, Billy Joe backed away to tug at his clothes. Carlos raised his hips, and his jeans slid down his legs, followed quickly by the removal of the rest of his clothes. Carlos moved backward up onto the bed as Billy Joe finished undressing and then climbed onto the bed, straddling him.

"What do you want?" Billy Joe asked, his lips close enough to feel the heat from his breath.

"You, all of you." Carlos wound his legs around Billy Joe's waist, holding his gaze with his own. He was more than ready. He reached to the nightstand, a foil packet glinting in the soft light. Carlos wanted to feel Billy Joe inside him, filling, stretching, completing. He groaned as Billy Joe prepared him, teasing and stretching until he got himself ready and slowly pressed into Carlos.

The heat that bloomed in Carlos's brain short-circuited his mind. He wanted this so bad, and yet it threatened to overwhelm him. He needed to remain in control to enjoy this and make it last. He hadn't been this close to the edge so quickly since he was a teenager.

Carlos turned his head away, burping softly, trying to cover it. He swallowed and burped again, this time louder. "Sorry."

Billy Joe snickered. "I was starting to wonder if you were going to belch Dixie." He raised his eyebrows, and Carlos lost it completely. He held Billy Joe to him as he laughed, carrying Billy Joe right along with him. God, that sound was glorious. Carlos ran his hands along Billy Joe's side. He meant to be sexy, but Billy Joe squirmed to get away, laughing harder. "I thought for a while I had forgotten how to do that." Billy Joe closed the distance between them, the laughter dying away as heat grew once again.

"Never forget how to laugh," Carlos told him seriously.

"But we were in the middle of...." Billy Joe tilted his head slightly.

"Sex should be passionate, but also joyful and happy." Carlos stroked Billy Joe's cheek. "The best sound I've heard in a long time was that laugh. You letting go of the fear and worry. It's like I get to see a new you. One without the cares and constant concerns weighing on you." Carlos leaned forward, bringing their lips together in a sloppy kiss.

"But we're naked and we're...." Billy Joe seemed almost scandalized, and Carlos didn't understand. "I mean, we're going to have sex...." His lips grew straight, his eyes hard. "This is serious. I just told you that I love you—"

"I love you too. I love it when your eyes are filled with passion." Carlos flicked his tongue over Billy Joe's lips. "I adore it when you let go and laugh." He kissed him, tugging gently on Billy Joe's lower lip. "I also love you when you're scared and don't seem to know where to turn. I don't like it when that happens, but I love you and will try to help. Good and bad, happy and sad, you can't have one without the other." Carlos ran his hands down Billy Joe's back.

"Oh...." Billy Joe grew quiet. "I wish I had fancy words to say how I felt...."

Carlos shook his head. "You already told me, remember? Those words were more than fancy enough for anyone." He wrapped his legs more tightly around Billy Joe. "Just be happy. That's what really counts." Carlos released his passion, surrendering his efforts to control himself, and gave over to Billy Joe. He'd ready many books on sex and relationships over the years, books on all types of thinking, and they had one thing in common: to get, you had to give, and the heart and brain were the most important sex organs of all. "That's all I want... to make you happy."

Some of the physicality had waned for a few minutes, but it returned with a vengeance. Billy Joe nodded, and Carlos pulled him forward, needing to join, to be together. "Slow and steady," Carlos whispered as Billy Joe pressed inside, pleasure following stretch and building to ecstasy.

"Is this what you meant?" Billy Joe panted, his eyes dilated. Carlos smiled, trying not to get lost in his own passion just so he could watch Billy Joe's.

"Oh yes." Carlos's heart beat like a drum, and he could feel Billy Joe's pulse deep inside him. It was an incredibly new sensation for him. To be in tune with someone so deeply, so completely, that Carlos's breathing synced with Billy Joe's as his body did, rocking slowly. They moved together, sighs building softly like ripples on a pond, cascading over one another. "That's it."

Billy Joe hummed softly in his ear. Carlos had no idea what the tune was, but it built in intensity by the second, adding to the intimacy of the moment, like their lovemaking had its own song that Billy Joe couldn't hold inside.

"God...."

"Yes...," Billy Joe whispered. "That's it. Just...." He stopped and leaned forward, kissing Carlos hard, pressing their hips together tightly. Billy Joe's cock flexed and bobbed inside him, sending Carlos into a high orbit that he never wanted to come down from. This was passion perfection. He clutched Billy Joe like a lifeline, not wanting this to end, and at the same time, afraid he was going to fly apart.

Billy Joe stopped, and Carlos tumbled back to earth. His head cleared and he blinked, wondering what had happened.

"Did you hear anything?"

"No." Billy Joe grinned wryly. "I just wanted to make sure you were still with me." He slowly pulled away and slid back inside in one long, slow motion.

"Oh," Carlos groaned, and prepared himself for the time of his life... and he wasn't disappointed for a second.

Control. A great word for so many things in life, and in the bedroom, Billy Joe seemed to be a master of it. He drove Carlos to the edge, pulled him back, and did it again so many times, he forgot how to see straight. Not that it mattered. At a time like this, seeing, thinking—those things were vastly overrated, and he went with it until he could take it no more. Every touch seemed hotter, more meaningful.

"Can't wait...," Carlos gasped as Billy Joe pressed him upward once again. His entire body shook with the need for release. Every cell screamed for it, and he wasn't going to be able to hold it back this time. Thankfully, Billy Joe had the same idea and didn't stop, pushing him higher and upward until lights danced behind his eyes and skyrockets crackled in his head.

His release was explosive, and he clung to Billy Joe as he followed right behind. They rocked, moaning softly together as they shook through it. Things like breathing and thinking were secondary. All that mattered was floating and being together, holding Billy Joe as they had the time of their lives.

"Jesus...," Carlos whimpered as his head stopped spinning, and he swallowed hard, a prone and warm Billy Joe on top of him. Now that was happiness in its purest, most amazing form.

CHAPTER 9

CHRISTMAS. BILLY Joe had sometimes wondered if he was going to make it through with his wits intact.

Tyler had been wound up as tight as a drum for a week beforehand. Every time he turned on the television, there was some kind of holiday special, and the toy commercials were unending. Tyler wanted everything he saw, and asked if Santa was coming a hundred million times. Billy Joe and Carlos had gotten a tree, and after Carlos strung the lights, they'd helped Tyler decorate it, with "lift me" becoming Tyler's favorite tree-trimming expression.

On Christmas Eve, all Billy Joe had wanted was a few hours of quiet, but Tyler stayed up until Carlos told him Santa wasn't going to come unless he was in bed. Tyler insisted on showing Santa his birthday tent, so he slept camping-style, which was becoming too common for Billy Joe's liking. He needed to do something about it but wasn't sure what to do at the moment.

"Santa been here!" had rung out at a godawful hour of the morning, and both he and Carlos groaned, hoping like heck that Tyler would sleep. They ate breakfast and then followed that with opening enough presents for a small army. Tyler made out like a bandit, thanks to Uncle Carlos. Then they'd all packed up and gone to Angie and Andy's for dinner. It had been a wonderful day, and when they got home, all three of them tumbled into bed, exhausted.

Now New Year's was fast approaching, and Billy Joe worked long hours between the holidays. There were a couple of dorms they were working to make repairs to, and they had a firm deadline. It was all right. Tyler and Carlos spent the days together, since Carlos didn't have to work until after the New Year. The thirtieth was Billy Joe's last day before the holiday, and he'd spent a few extra hours at work. They finished painting the hallways and putting the light fixture covers back into place.

A light snow fell all day, and by the time he got home, it had nearly stopped, but everything was covered in a blanket of white. As he trudged up the shoveled walk, he couldn't help smiling at the snow angels in the front yard, some big, some small. It seemed someone had been playing outside. He pulled open the front door, went inside, and closed it, cutting off the flow of cold air.

"Some faggot wetback is not going to stop me from seeing my grandson!"

That voice sent ice running up his spine. He'd be better off back outside as old, conditioned fear raced through him. He forced his legs to work, trudging up the stairs to where his mother stood outside Carlos's open door. He took a deep breath. It was now or never. He'd always worried that things would come to this, but he hadn't expected his mother to be the one to show up at his door.

"We don't talk like that around here," he said as he reached the top of the stairs.

Tyler raced out of the apartment and into his arms, tears running down his cheeks. "Gran and Uncle Carlos are fighting." He raised his arms, and Billy Joe lifted him and held him closely. "And Gran cussed and was mean." He buried his head on Billy Joe's shoulder.

"Tell him to stay away from my grandson!" his mother screeched, her hair going in all directions as she pointed at Carlos.

"First thing, I left Tyler with Carlos while I was working. He had my permission to be with Tyler. And secondly, that kind of hate speech will not be tolerated here. If you can't be civil, you can leave." It was Billy Joe's turn to point.

"Don't talk to me like that. I brought you into this world—I can take you out of it."

Aggression washed off his mother as she stepped close to him. He'd seen that look before, and it usually preceded one of her corporal punishment phases. Years of ingrained behavior took over, and he needed a few seconds to recognize and overrule the Pavlovian response.

Her hand clenched into a fist. "So help me, Billy Joe. I have your father in jail because he couldn't stick to the damn rules, and I spent the holidays alone, without my grandson. Then I track you down and come up here, and I find Tyler with this—"

"That's enough!" Billy Joe snapped. He stepped toward Carlos, turned, and spoke quietly. "Please take him into your apartment. My mother and I are going to talk, and I don't want him hearing this." He passed Tyler to him. "It's okay, sweetheart. Uncle Carlos will have a snack for you, and I'll be right over."

"Don't you dare—" His mother reached for Tyler, but Billy Joe stepped between her and Carlos.

"I mean it." Billy Joe needed to keep cool. Once Carlos had gone inside and the door was closed, he turned on his mother.

"I'll call the police," she threatened. "I have a right to see my grandson."

Billy Joe pulled out his phone. "You have no rights whatsoever as far as Tyler is concerned. So go ahead. You've made threats and yelled. I'm certain there are other witnesses. Maybe we can throw your ass in jail, and you can sit there for a while, because I sure as hell ain't bailing you out." He opened the door to his apartment, and they went inside to ensure Tyler couldn't hear.

As soon as the door closed, she tried again. "What the hell were you thinking, taking Tyler like that in the middle of the goddamned night? Leaving your family and everything. We looked for both of you for days and called the police. No note… not shit! There's no excuse for that."

"Sure there is." Billy Joe had to clamp his mouth shut to keep from yelling at the top of his lungs. "I didn't want my son around you and Dad any longer. He's a sweet little boy who deserves a better life than the hate-filled, piece-of-shit one you gave me." He saw the blow coming and grabbed her arm, clenching it in his fist.

150

"That's enough of that shit, Mother." He released her. "Go ahead, try it again. That's assault, and you can rot in jail."

"He's my grandson," she seethed.

"And he's my son, and I will decide who can see him and who can't. I'm not having my sheet-wearing father and useless mother around him any longer. We came here to get away from you, your friends, and everything they stand for."

The door opened behind him and Carlos peered inside. "You okay?" Just like that, the nerves that had been just under the surface, threatening to undermine his determination, flew away, like a flake of snow in a gale. "Tyler is watching Daniel Tiger with a cookie and some milk. I just wanted to check on you."

Billy Joe took a deep breath and released it. "I'm fine." It was a lie, but he wasn't going to let his mother see how upset he was. "I'll be over in a little while."

Carlos closed the door, and Billy Joe motioned to one of the chairs. "Sit down."

His mother looked as though she wasn't sure she wanted to.

"It's up to you." He sat on the sofa and waited.

"Your father and I did our best for you," she began. It was an old tune, and one that rang hollow. She lowered herself to the chair.

"Yes. You showed me the people I should hate and make fun of." Billy Joe leaned forward. "Well, I'm one of those people. Did that ever occur to you? I'm gay, Mom. Carlos and I are in a relationship, and I love him." He hardened his gaze as she grew paler than the snow outside. He was aware of her argument and headed it off. "And I don't care what you think about it. Not one little bit. Your hate-tainted opinion is less than worthless. That's why I left. I was tired of hating myself and the person I was when I was around you. There was no way I was ever going to be able to stop hiding."

"I'll fight you in court. That's no way to raise Tyler." Her eyes damn near burned red.

151

Billy Joe had known this was coming. His father had given it away on the phone. "Try. We don't live in Mississippi any longer. You'd have to file suit here. Tyler is my son. I don't have to let you see him or ever return to Jackson. That threat is as hollow as Dad's head. And as for raising Tyler, I'm his father and that's final." He was getting to the end of his patience. God in heaven, he saw clearly just how bad things had been at home and what he'd put up with all these years.

"You have answers for everything, don't you?" She smirked.

"You and Dad had plenty of answers for years, and they were all shit."

She jumped to her feet. "Don't you dare sass me. I'm your mother and you owe me some respect."

Billy Joe stayed where he was. "Respect is earned, not given, and you've done nothing to earn it... nothing at all. You raised me in an environment where I heard how terrible everyone was but white people. Remember Dad taking me to a cross-burning when I was ten? What kind of parenting is that? And you were no better. Well, now it's all come back to roost. Dad's going to go to prison for a very long time, and so are a lot of his friends. And any money the group has is going to be siphoned away by legal bills and judgments."

She fell back into the chair. Billy Joe could feel the anger leaching out of her. "I raised you the way I was raised."

"With stupidity and hate. But I will not raise Tyler the way you did me. It ends here. I'm a different person, more caring, and I will raise him with love, not hate and fear." Billy Joe plowed forward. "If in the future you can leave all that behind, then maybe you can be part of Tyler's life in some way. But Dad never will be. He blew that when he encouraged the shooting of...."

Shit. He'd been trying to avoid bringing up any details.

"Who have you been talking to?" She sat up straighter. "Boy?"

"Who do you think? I'm his son. You think they aren't going to call me? I left town, remember?" Billy Joe realized now that it wasn't going to be too hard for his mother to put things together based on the timing, but he didn't care anymore. "The thing is, it's best if Tyler never sees or talks to him again. Let that relationship die. Lord knows I'm not ever visiting that old goat in prison. And your relationship with him is up to you."

"What? You think I'm going to stand by while my grandson is raised by the parade of sissy men you have running through your bedroom? No way in hell." Her defiance was back.

"Then we're done." Billy Joe stood and walked to the door. "Leave and don't come back. If you do, I will have you arrested for trespassing and threatening me and my son." He leaned out the door. "Did you hear that, Carlos?"

"Yup."

"So I have a witness." Billy Joe glared at her.

"Where am I supposed to go? It's snowing and cold. I...." His mother suddenly seemed so much smaller than she had only a few minutes earlier.

"Find a hotel and stay there on your way back south. Go home, back to what you know. Forget about me and Tyler. I'm never going to be the son you want." He waited until she stepped into the hall and closed the door. "Tyler, come say goodbye to Gran," he said softly after opening Carlos's door.

Tyler came out slowly, peeking around the corner. "You still yelling?"

Billy Joe knelt down. "Your grandma and I had some things we needed to talk about, and I'm sorry if you heard us yelling." It was the way his mother and father had of getting their point across. They yelled louder than the next guy, and usually their opponent simply gave up.

"Don't lie to him. Your father doesn't want me to see you because—"

Billy Joe glared at her and waved his hand in front of her face. "That's enough, Mother. Either behave or go." He wasn't going to put up with her upsetting Tyler. This was going to be difficult

153

enough to explain as it was. "Tyler is your grandson, and he isn't party to what's between us." Hopefully that was something she could understand.

He nodded to Tyler, and he hurried to her. Billy Joe's mother lifted him up, rocking back and forth. She loved Tyler in her own way, Billy Joe knew that, but having her in his life was something he just couldn't allow anymore. Not with how things were at the moment.

Carlos stood behind him, lightly touching his shoulder. It was just enough that he knew Carlos was there.

She kissed Tyler's cheek and turned. Billy Joe tensed, prepared to chase after his mother if she decided to run. He understood that her world had been turned on its ear and so many of the things she thought she understood had been ripped away from her.

"Mother," Billy Joe said, cautioning, and she set Tyler down. "You can go watch cartoons with Uncle Carlos. I'll be in with you in a few minutes."

Carlos followed Tyler inside and closed the door. With him safe, Billy Joe approached his mother. "I won't go over everything again. You are my mother. However, things need to change if you're going to be part of either Tyler's or my life." He kept his voice level and calm, but it was damn hard. "This hateful shit must end. Tyler will not be raised around that, and it will not be part of my life either."

She grimaced and muttered under her breath. Billy Joe couldn't understand what she was saying, but it was becoming crystal clear that she wasn't going to be able to change. And that hurt.

"You expect me to bend to what you want?"

Billy Joe sighed. "No. I'm saying that you're free to live your life any way you want. But from your reaction, you'll need to get used to not seeing Tyler. He loves you, and so do I, in a way." He wasn't sure what he was trying to say. "For a while I think it's best that he and I go on with our lives."

A crocodile tear ran down her cheek. "You're really going to keep my only grandchild away from me?"

Billy Joe nodded. "I won't bring him up the way you did me. I don't want that influence." He stepped closer, and her eyes widened. "Do you really think you can accept me as a gay man and the fact that I want to live my life with Carlos?" He tilted his head slightly. "All of that is up to you. But I won't be disrespected or belittled." He stepped back. "Have a safe trip home." Any thought that he might have had about his mother somehow accepting him to a degree was a fantasy that he had to let go of. His mother was never going to change, not even for her own grandson.

She disappeared down the stairs, and the outside door closed. Billy Joe stayed still, watching after her for a few seconds before turning around and entering the apartment. His old family, his blood family, the last of them, had just walked out the door, and the door was closed. His parents were never going to set aside their deeply held beliefs for him or anyone else.

"Daddy." Tyler ran over and hugged his legs. "You look sad."

Billy Joe nodded. "I am." He knelt down. "Come give me a hug and make it all better." Tyler threw his arms around Billy Joe's neck, making squeezy noises. "That's just what I needed." He released Tyler and smiled. "You always make me feel happy."

Tyler ran back to the sofa, climbed up, and settled in to watch the program.

"Are you really okay?" Carlos asked quietly.

"Not really." There was no use covering it up. "I know you went through this same thing, and I shouldn't let myself feel this way...."

Carlos hugged him. "You've lost something important to most of us. And you know it isn't coming back. You need to grieve for it."

"But they aren't dead."

"They might as well be. You aren't going to exchange phone calls, and they aren't going to be there for you or Tyler in any way. I had to go through this to some extent. I can tell you it's hard not to hold on to that last thread of hope that they'll change and decide you're worth it."

Billy Joe understood and nodded. "They never will. I'm not worth it to them—I never was. They will always think of me as someone less than they are." He sighed. "I guess I need to keep reminding myself why I left in the first place." It was foolish of him to think there was anything salvageable in the relationship. It was over, and that was the end of it.

"It's okay to be angry, upset, and even sad. But you're a better person than they are."

Carlos was right, but what could Billy Joe do about it? Not fucking much.

"It still hurts." Even though he probably had no reason to. He was the one who left in the first place.

Tyler slid down from the sofa as his program ended. "Uncle Carlos, I'm hungry." He looked up at them, lower lip sticking out as he did his best to make that pathetic, "take pity on me" face.

Carlos scooped him up and made plane sounds as he flew Tyler around the room, to high-pitched giggles that should have made Billy Joe smile. Instead, he left them alone and went into the kitchen. There was no need for him to bring both of them down. He stared at the refrigerator door, intending to see what was for dinner, but he didn't even open it, a field of white, static and still in front of him. God, he hated white.

"Daddy." Tyler tugged at his pant leg, and Billy Joe turned to him, wiping the wet tracks off his cheeks.

"Hey, buddy," he said with as much forced enthusiasm as he could muster.

"Go on and sit down. Tyler and I are going to make dinner," Carlos said.

"I help," Tyler squealed with excitement.

Billy Joe went and sat on the sofa. He wasn't going to be any good to anyone at the moment and needed to get out of the way. There was nothing anyone else could do for him. He needed to deal with this on his own. And fuck it all to hell, Billy Joe wished things had turned out very differently. *Hell, if wishes were candy, we'd all have a Merry Christmas.* That's what his grandmother used to say. She'd been referring to those childish wishes that seemed so important at the time, but in the grand scheme of things, had meant very little. Now he understood what the saying truly meant. He could wish for anything he wanted, including his parents to be the people he wanted them to be and felt he deserved, but they weren't going to change, and he needed to get the fuck over it, fast.

"I wanna do it," Tyler said from the kitchen.

"You will. But I need to get you ready." Carlos was so patient with him. "Is that good?"

"Yeah." A giggle followed, and Billy Joe sighed softly.

Shit and blast. Here he was, sitting alone, when the rest of his family….

That thought, those words, took him aback for a few seconds. Was it possible that the family he'd been born with had been replaced so quickly? Carlos had stepped into his life with acceptance and support. Could things really be that easy and work that well?

Billy Joe stood up and wandered over to the table so he could peer into the kitchen. Tyler had a dish towel around his waist, and he stood at the counter, ripping up pieces of lettuce one leaf at a time and placing them in a colander. Billy Joe smiled, watching Tyler as he worked, so serious, as though each piece of lettuce and every movement he made were extremely important.

Carlos noticed him and stepped back from the stove to give Billy Joe a quick kiss before returning to what he was doing.

"I make salad, Daddy," Tyler said, bouncing a little on the stool.

"Be careful as you help Uncle Carlos."

Tyler nodded, returning his attention to what he was doing. Carlos winked at him and continued stirring.

"What are we having?"

"I'm making mole. I bought a jar of the good stuff at the store today, and I have the chicken almost ready to go in."

"Moldies," Tyler said. "Ewww."

"Not moldies, mole. It's a really good sauce with chocolate in it." Billy Joe figured that would at least get Tyler to try it. He tickled Tyler a little, steadying him so he didn't fall as he giggled. "We don't eat moles." He hugged him. "You're getting a little silly." He let Tyler return to his work and figured it was best if he stayed out of the way. Billy Joe wasn't exactly sure what he should be doing, so he wandered through the apartment and ended up back on the sofa, turning on the television but not really watching anything.

Tyler barreled into him, taking him by the hand. "It's time to eat," he said earnestly, tugging him up. "I'm hungry and the moles is ready." Tyler pulled him to the table, and Carlos brought in the food and the salad. Tyler looked so proud, beaming over the large bowl. "I helped." He pointed to the salad, and Carlos helped him dish some out to each of them. Then Tyler climbed in his booster seat, and they sat down to eat.

"Have you made a resolution for the New Year?" Carlos asked as he placed a small piece of chicken on Tyler's plate. Billy Joe cut it up, and Tyler took a tentative bite. He must have liked it because he picked up his fork and dug right in.

"Not really. I have until tomorrow, right?" Billy Joe asked. He wasn't in the mood for resolutions or anything else. He was having a pity party of one and wasn't ready to let the damn thing come to an end.

"How about you? What do you want to do for the New Year?" Carlos asked Tyler.

"I want a horse. He could stay with me in my room. I could feed him hay and ride him outside." Tyler practically bounced in his seat.

"I don't think there's enough room in the apartment for a horse. But resolutions are things you want to do, not presents like Christmas. Maybe a good resolution for you is to grow big enough that you can use a big-boy chair like your daddy and me," Carlos offered.

"And not eat yucky stuff." Tyler furrowed his tiny brow, and Billy Joe had to keep himself from laughing. The resolutions of three-year-olds were so immediate.

"Okay," Billy Joe humored him. Tyler wasn't a picky eater, but there were a few things he refused to have anything to do with, including cauliflower and broccoli. "Tomorrow is New Year's Eve, and we're going to Auntie Angie's for a party." Not that Tyler would actually stay up that late, but it would give him something to look forward to.

"Gran too?" Tyler asked.

Billy Joe shook his head. "Gran went back home." He was at a loss for words as to how to explain things to him. Billy Joe hated that he had to keep Tyler and his mother apart, but he didn't have much choice. In the long run, it would be better for Tyler.

"No." Tyler hopped off his seat and ran toward the door. "Gran!" he cried loudly, reaching up to pull on the doorknob, shaking it in his little hands.

Billy Joe hurried over and lifted Tyler up, Tyler fighting and kicking the entire time.

"I want Gran."

"I know. But she's gone now." Billy Joe stroked his back, rocking him as he paced.

"But I just want Gran." Tyler's temper had dissipated to tears, and Billy Joe did his best to soothe him. He wasn't going to lie to him and make promises he couldn't keep.

"Tomorrow night you're going to see Auntie Angie and Uncle Andy and go to a party. There will be good food and lots of fun, and we can watch the big ball drop in New York to usher in the New Year." How in the heck did he explain that this was just an artificial holiday strictly based on the clock... and an excuse for a final party before going back to work after a midwinter break? "You'll have fun."

Tyler sniffled and rested his head on Billy Joe's shoulder. "I want Gran," he whined, and Billy Joe continued soothing him as guilt rose higher and higher.

Eventually Tyler calmed down, and Billy Joe got him back to the table. He picked at his food, and Billy Joe didn't have the heart to try to coax him to eat.

"Why don't I take you home and you can have a bath and go to bed?" Billy Joe was so tired that he just wanted to get Tyler to sleep, and then he could lie down and try to put this awful day behind him.

"Daniel Tiger," Tyler said pathetically, and Billy didn't argue with him. He was coming to the end of his patience and didn't want to yell. Thankfully, Carlos flew Tyler into the living room, got him a pillow and blanket, and found an on-demand episode. Tyler curled under the blanket, peering out as he watched the television. Carlos turned down the lights and then went into the kitchen.

Billy Joe helped him clean up dinner and put the leftovers away. "I'm sorry."

"What for?" Carlos asked. "Because you've been through hell and back because of your family and you aren't feeling like a bundle of hearts and puppies?" He shrugged. "So what? You're allowed." He finished cleaning up and turned out the kitchen lights.

By the time they were done, Tyler was asleep on the sofa. Billy Joe turned down the television and lowered the last of the lights. Tyler didn't wake, and eventually he rolled over toward the back of the sofa, continuing to sleep.

"I hate to move him." Billy Joe didn't want to wake him up for any reason. He didn't blame Tyler for being upset. He just wanted his gran.

"Then don't. You can stay with me, and if he wakes up, you'll be here." Carlos changed the channel, but Tyler didn't stir.

They watched a couple episodes of *Top Chef* before turning off the television. Carlos went into the spare bedroom and returned with the night-light Tyler used when he was "camping." Carlos plugged it in nearby, and they went into the bedroom, closing the door.

"I feel like I'm taking advantage of you," Billy Joe said as he sat on the side of the bed. "I spend so much of my time over here, and you do most of the cooking for both of us."

"Hey, I like having you here, and you help out plenty." Carlos sat next to him. "I've been thinking that maybe it would be best if we talked to Mrs. C to see when one of the larger apartments on the first floor will become available. She has two three-bedroom units. Each is half the first floor. She lives in one, and I heard the family in the other is moving soon. So maybe the three of us could move in there together. It would be less expensive than what we're paying here combined. Tyler would have his own room, and the extra bedroom could be an office or playroom, and maybe some storage. We could get Tyler a toybox, and he'd have a place for his things."

"Are you sure about this?" Billy Joe hadn't thought of something like that at all. "I mean, it's not like I don't want to, but living with me and Tyler is…."

Carlos scoffed. "You do realize that you and Tyler have spent most of your nights here for the last few weeks? In reality you've been living here, and I like having both of you around." Carlos put an arm around his shoulders, tugging him closer.

As Billy Joe turned to look at Carlos, he leaned nearer, eliminating the distance between them. Carlos kissed him, hugging Billy Joe tightly, deepening their embrace. Billy Joe gave himself over. He only wanted to be happy, and he had no doubt that being with Carlos would do just that.

CARLOS HELD him all night in a warm, comforting embrace that Billy Joe hadn't even known he needed.

"Daddy!"

The cry went right up his spine, and Billy Joe jumped, nearly pushing Carlos to the floor as he struggled to get out of bed. It was still dark, and he had no idea what time it was. Carlos groaned as Billy Joe yanked on his pants and hurried out of the room.

He found Tyler standing on the cushions, looking out the window, staring. "What is it?"

"The monsters were trying to get in," Tyler said, turning around.

Billy Joe sat next to him on the sofa. "Do you see any of them now?"

Tyler climbed on his lap. "No. Just the tree." He leaned against him.

"Did you have a bad dream?" Billy Joe asked, rocking slowly back and forth. "It's okay. I have bad dreams too sometimes, and I get scared."

Tyler lifted his gaze upward. "You, Daddy?" The expression of disbelief touched Billy Joe's heart. Like his daddy was too big and strong to be scared of anything.

Billy Joe nodded. "I get scared too. Mostly of anything ever happening to you." He hugged Tyler closer, continuing to rock him slowly. "What was the dream about?"

Tyler yawned and leaned on him, not answering. Hopefully, whatever it was, the memory was fading away already. Tyler was already falling back to sleep.

Billy Joe was familiar with nightmares. He'd had them for many years and had to deal with them. The subject of most of them was his own damn family. Billy Joe hummed softly, singing his son back to sleep, and then gently laid him on the sofa, covered him up, and kissed him on the forehead. He peeked through the curtains, but only saw the tree in the side yard and flakes of snow falling silently to the ground. He closed the curtains and returned to the bedroom, undressed, and got back into bed.

"Nightmare?"

"Yeah." Billy Joe sighed, and Carlos snuggled in, warming him up again.

"The real nightmares are behind. You know that… for both of you." Carlos slid his hand across Billy Joe's chest, tugging him a little closer. Billy Joe rolled over, and Carlos pressed to his back. Neither of them made a move toward sex. This was exactly what Billy Joe needed. Someone to hold him when the nightmares came, and they probably would for him, just like they had for Tyler.

"I hope so." But he certainly wasn't holding out much hope.

"They are because you've put them behind you." Carlos stroked his belly, and Billy Joe hummed happily. "You did that. Not anyone else. You got out and were strong enough to decide the kind of life you wanted for you and Tyler."

"Yeah. But at what cost? I never want to see my mom and dad again. And I can live with that. But Tyler deserves good grandparent figures who are part of his life, even if they don't share blood."

The more he thought about it, the more he realized that was a lie. He wished his parents were worthy of being in Tyler's life, but that was never going to happen. His parents were never going to turn into people he could allow in their lives. That was a fact he had to deal with, and the nightmare of what he'd witnessed and the years of living in fear… well, they were a small price to pay for their true safety and peace of mind. Lord knew he'd never go back to living that way.

"Go back to sleep. You're thinking way too much for four in the morning." Carlos yawned behind him. "Besides, the answer for that is easy. Just get Tyler new grandparents." He snuffled softly and stilled, his breathing steadying as he fell back to sleep.

Billy Joe wished the solution to the problem were that simple.

EVENTUALLY HE fell to sleep and woke to giggles coming from the other room.

"Daddy!" Tyler burst into the room. "Uncle Carlos and I made cakes." He jumped onto the bed, and Billy Joe snatched him into a hug that ended with more giggles. "Come eat."

"Okay. Go on out with Uncle Carlos and I'll be right there." He got up as Tyler jumped off the bed and raced into the other room.

"It snowed. Can we go out and play in it?" Tyler asked.

"You want to make snow angels again?" Carlos asked.

Billy Joe found his pants and pulled them on. He finished dressing and joined the others. Tyler climbed into his seat, and Carlos brought the food to the table. As he sat down, Billy Joe realized that this was what a family should look like.

"Daddy, sit here." Tyler pointed to one side of him. "Uncle Carlos, here."

"I'll be there in just a minute." Billy Joe helped Carlos with the juice and brought the syrup and butter to the table. Then they all sat down to a New Year's Eve morning breakfast. "Maybe this year will be better. What do you think?"

Tyler blinked at him as he shoved a bite of pancake in his mouth. Clearly, he was happy.

"Do you want the paper?" Carlos asked, pulling open the door to head down to get it. He stopped and stared. "Billy Joe." Carlos turned, confused.

Billy Joe joined him. He stared at a small pile of presents outside his apartment door in various Christmas wrappings. He went over, picked up the five wrapped gifts, and checked the tags.

They all were for Tyler from his parents. His mother must have returned and left them. There was no additional note, just the gifts.

"What do you want to do?" Carlos asked.

"We'll give them to Tyler later." Billy Joe unlocked the door and put the gifts inside his apartment. "Let's go finish breakfast." He would figure out what to do later. As much as he wanted his parents to be good people, that wasn't necessarily the case. They were who they were and a product of their upbringing, just like so many of the others he knew, but that didn't excuse their actions or their inability to take responsibility for them.

"You don't need to feel guilty." Carlos took his hand and said no more.

Billy Joe paused at the open apartment door. "How did you know?"

"Because I felt guilty for a long time. I wondered if things with my family were my fault. Maybe if I'd been different or more understanding or… maybe if I tried harder to work things out with them. But their attitudes aren't going to change no matter what, and your parents aren't going to accept or even respect you." Carlos led him back inside.

Tyler was still in his seat, looking up as they came in. "You leaved me," he said, pushing out his lower lip.

Billy Joe hurried around to him. "We were just outside, and we didn't forget about you." He ruffled Tyler's hair. "I see you finished your breakfast." Billy Joe cleaned him up and helped Tyler down. "You can watch television for a little while, and then you and I will go home and you can change your clothes." Billy Joe finished his breakfast, which had gotten a little cold, and then carried his dishes to the sink, thanked Carlos, and carried Tyler home so they could get ready for what was going to be a late night for both of them.

"Daniel Tiger," Tyler whined as he brought him across the hall. When he saw the presents, Tyler rushed over to them, so Billy Joe placed them on the floor and let Tyler open the presents from

Gran. Tyler was happy, settling in to play with his new Legos and Lincoln Logs.

Billy Joe went through to the bathroom once he turned on the television and found something to help keep Tyler occupied while he took a shower.

The water felt good, but he didn't have a chance to enjoy it. He only had enough time to wash and rinse before jumping out to get dressed and rejoining Tyler, who hadn't moved from in front of the television. "Buddy, do you want to have your bath? Then you can watch television for a while again." He hadn't had a chance to bathe the night before, and Billy Joe wanted Tyler to clean up and change his clothes.

He got Tyler undressed and into the tub, playing with his toys. He thought he heard Carlos and cracked the door.

"Billy Joe?"

"Hey." Billy Joe didn't want to step away, so he poked his head out of the door.

"Angie called, and there will be some other people at the party tonight. Her mom and dad had plans that fell through, so they're coming."

"Okay." It wasn't like Billy Joe had anything to say about who came to the party.

"Hi, buddy. You playing boats?" Carlos asked as Tyler splashed and laughed.

"What's going on?" Billy Joe asked, turning to look back to Tyler, who was still playing happily.

"Nothing." Carlos kissed him. "I was just a little lonely."

Why that tickled him so much was a little surprising. "Tyler and I will be out in a few minutes, and he can play for a while." Billy Joe closed the door and helped Tyler finish his bath. Once Tyler was dressed, he played on the living room floor while Billy Joe sat on the sofa with Carlos.

"I don't know what to do about my mom. Dad is done after what he did…." Billy Joe turned to Tyler, who was making a house out of his Lincoln Logs.

"Why don't you give it some time? Give yourself a break and let yourself have a little fun. Both Tyler and you deserve that." Carlos put his arm around him, and Billy Joe leaned into the touch. It was amazing how easily he had come to rely on Carlos, who he was quickly coming to think of as the librarian of his heart. He didn't want to leave, and it also didn't seem to bother either of them that they were watching Daniel Tiger, yet again.

The more Billy Joe thought about it, the more he realized that Carlos was right. He needed to put some distance between him and his mother and let things cool down for a while. Once he could think, he'd figure out what to do… if anything. Right now it was time for him to spend time with his new family.

Billy Joe angled his face upward, and Carlos closed the distance between them.

"Daddy, kissing…," Tyler said in a naughty tone before giggling.

Carlos slid off the sofa onto the floor to play Legos with Tyler. Billy Joe joined them after a few minutes. He put together the race car set his mother had bought for Tyler. Once it was together, Billy Joe sat at the table with a tablet to write his mother a letter. While he was playing with Tyler, he'd realized he had a lot to say to his mom and decided it was best to write down his thoughts.

"SWEETHEART," CARLOS said later, pulling him out of his thoughts. Billy Joe had half a dozen handwritten pages on the table, his hand cramping a little as he set down his pen. "We should get ready to go."

"Okay." He'd put down so many thoughts and needed to review them later, but he'd gotten them down and now they could exist on paper, rather than running through his head. "I think I can let things go for now."

Carlos encircled Billy Joe in his arms, pressing a cheek to his.

Billy Joe pushed away the papers, letting Carlos's comfort and warmth sink deep into him. "Do we really have to go?" He wasn't being serious, but he was really happy right where he was.

Carlos chuckled. Neither of them would think of staying home after they had agreed to come.

"Ready to go see Auntie Angie?" Billy Joe asked Tyler, who jumped up and ran into the bedroom. He came out with one shoe on and his coat on inside out. "Come here, honey." Billy Joe slipped out of Carlos's arms and helped Tyler out of his coat. "Go ahead and put your toys away, and then I'll help you get your shoes and coat on."

Tyler groaned. "I wanna go see Auntie."

"I know. So put your toys away." Billy Joe had to be firm, and Tyler moved slowly, dragging his feet as though the toys weighed a ton, but he did get his toys put away. "You should get ready too. It's going to take me a little while to get him moving."

Carlos kissed him and left while Billy Joe got Tyler's things together for the night.

"You can take two toys with you. Put them in this bag. Just two." Billy Joe held up his fingers, and Tyler put in a stuffed dog and then tried to push in the entire tube of Lincoln Logs. "How about one of your books? That would be better."

Tyler huffed as though he was completely put out, but got *Goodnight Moon*, and Billy Joe added one of the small Lego kits to the bag. Once the rest of the toys were put away, he helped Tyler get both shoes on the correct feet.

Then Billy Joe got himself ready. It was hard when Tyler demanded his attention the minute he left the room. By the time he returned to the living room—he could've sworn he was only gone two minutes—all the Legos were strewn around the room and Tyler sat in the middle of them, playing. "We're going to go, so put them all away." Billy Joe sat down, getting impatient and trying not to let his temper take over. He needed to take the time to make sure Tyler understood he needed to put his own things away.

Nearly a half hour later, he and Tyler were ready and going over to Carlos's. He came out right away, and they left the building. Billy Joe drove, and Carlos directed him across town to near the university.

"We going to Auntie Angie's?"

"Yes, buddy," Billy Joe answered as he pulled up in front of a tidy, two-story brick home with classical white columns in front. "We're here." He parked, and Carlos helped Tyler out while Billy Joe grabbed all their stuff and did his best imitation of a pack mule as he approached the door. Tyler's bag was stuffed because he'd brought an extra change of clothes, as well as pajamas for him.

"Hi, guys," Andy said at the door, taking one of the bags as Billy Joe approached. "Come on in. Angie has been cooking up a storm." He took coats and set the bag near the living room door. "There are appetizers on the coffee table, and Angie made you something special," he said to Tyler, who stared in the living room at the Christmas tree that rose to the ceiling. Tyler ran over, looking up at the lights.

"Come on," Billy Joe said, holding out his hand. He waited for Tyler to take it and then knelt down. "There's lots of pretty things here. Just be sure to ask before you touch anything that isn't yours." He led Tyler to the sofa, sat down, and lifted Tyler on his lap. The house was filled with small items and art pieces.

"Sweetheart," Angie said as she set down a plate of bruschetta. She took Tyler's hand, guiding him off his lap, and led him away toward the kitchen. "I got some special food for you that Uncle Carlos said you really liked."

The front door opened, and Andy jumped up, hellos sounding through the hall, and then an older couple entered and Billy Joe stood. "This is Angie's mom and dad, Sue and Ronald."

Billy Joe shook hands and jumped as a squeal rang from the other room. Tyler ran in holding a bowl filled with strawberries in both hands. He came to a stop near Billy Joe, handing him the bowl.

"Sweetie, this is my daddy and mommy," Angie said.

"Hi." Sue knelt down. "You're really handsome, aren't you?" She smiled, and Tyler nodded. "You look a lot like your daddy."

"This is Tyler. Can you say hi?"

Tyler pressed close to Billy Joe and said nothing for a few seconds.

Sue reached into a paper bag and handed Tyler a wrapped present. Suddenly he was Mr. Personable, ripping the paper off a sticker book. He grinned and said thank you.

"Do you want to do stickers with me?" Sue asked, holding out her hand, and Tyler took it. "We'll be in the other room." She pointed across the hall, and Tyler went right with her, talking up a blue streak.

"Don't forget your berries," Billy Joe said, taking the berries in to them. Sue already had Tyler settled at a table with the book open.

"Dinosaurs, Daddy!" Tyler showed him the book before sitting right down. Sue took the spot next to him with a smile.

"It's been a while since we've had little ones around." The longing in her voice was hard to miss. She probably wanted to be a grandmother very badly. "Tyler and I will be good for a while." She patted his shoulder. "It's fine if you want to go in and enjoy the party. He and I are going to be good friends."

Somehow Billy Joe didn't doubt her for a second. "Thank you." He left the two of them to their book and rejoined the others.

Angie had joined the small group in the living room, setting down a tray of what she said were Sazeracs. Billy Joe sat next to Carlos on the sofa, sighing softly. It seemed it was just the seven of them for the evening.

"Sue is already talking about moving here," Ron was saying. "She's determined to be closer to her new grandchild, and I can't blame her." The sad pall that crept over his features was hard to miss.

Carlos leaned closer. "Angie's older brother, Johnny, and his wife, Betsy, had a baby about eight years ago, and he passed away when he was Tyler's age. Betsy wasn't able to have any more children." He spoke very quietly, and Billy Joe nodded his understanding.

"She's already been checking the real estate markets and wants to look at houses after the first of the year. I explained that the best time to look was in the spring, but she is so anxious and wants to be here when the baby is born."

Giggling drifted in from the other room, and then Tyler raced in with his sticker book. "Look, Daddy," he said, showing him the page. "Gramma Sue and I did it. Rawr!" He made dinosaur noises and then showed Carlos. "We make more." He raced out to the other room.

"I wish I had his energy," Ron commented.

"Gramma Sue?" Billy Joe asked Carlos.

"Does it bother you? I can tell Mother—" Angie began.

"No," Billy Joe answered. He kinda liked it.

Angie shifted, leaning back as though she were trying to get comfortable. "I know it's early, but dang, I swear this baby is already pressing on my back and sitting on my bladder most of the time." She seemed to settle and then dug into the snacks as though she were starving. "When Carlos first joined the university staff, he was alone—"

Carlos scoffed. "That's an understatement. I didn't know anyone, and the first day on the job, this tall, thin, gorgeous creature walked into my office and perched herself on the corner of my desk, introduced herself, and asked me to lunch."

"I just knew we were going to be friends," Angie said, "and after that, we became family. I was lucky because I have Mom and Dad, and when they first met Carlos, they sort of adopted him. And now I think Mom has her sights on Tyler."

Billy Joe sighed again. "It isn't like he's going to be able to spend time with his real grandparents any longer. It's just not possible." It was simply a fact that he needed to live with. He really didn't want to talk about them any longer. It wasn't worth it.

Ron reached for a tortilla chip and dipped it in a meat-and-cheese concoction that smelled like heaven. Billy Joe got one for himself. Man, that dip was good, with just enough heat and spice to be interesting. "How a parent can turn their back on a child for no reason other than them being different is beyond me," Ron said as he reached for another chip.

"I knew they could never accept it. That's why we left." Billy Joe hadn't wanted to bring this up tonight, but it seemed it was out of his hands.

"You can't pick your family, so thank God you can pick your friends," Andy chimed in, and then hastened on. "But it's even better when your family can become friends."

"Nice save, sweetheart," Angie chirped and sipped from her glass of orange juice.

"But it's true. I'm making my own family with you." Andy beamed and gently rubbed Angie's belly. He was going to be the proudest new father in the state at this rate.

Billy Joe leaned over toward Carlos, their shoulders bumping lightly, and Carlos entwined their fingers between them, squeezing lightly. Somehow Billy Joe figured this entire conversation had been engineered for his benefit. But he was finally ready to accept that he had to let go of his birth family, the one that was never going to work or accept him, so he could build one of his own with Carlos. And that was what he wanted.

"Can we talk to Mrs. C next week?" Billy Joe asked, and Carlos grinned, the sun rising in his smile.

"You bet." Carlos lifted his glass, and Billy Joe lightly clinked it with his. He sipped and then sat back, as content as he could remember being.

Dinner was roast pork with potatoes and roasted vegetables. Afterward, Billy Joe got Tyler changed into his pajamas, and Angie brought down some blankets for him. Tyler nearly fell asleep in his arms, and Billy Joe carried him into the other room. At Tyler's insistence, his "Gramma Sue" read him *Goodnight Moon*, and then he was out for the evening.

They talked and laughed until it was nearly midnight, turning on the television to watch the ball drop in Times Square. The television grew louder as the excitement for the New Year built.

Tyler padded in, wearing his green dinosaur footy pajamas, rubbing his eyes. Billy Joe lifted him on his lap, and Tyler snuggled right in. "It's going to be New Year's soon."

At the stroke of midnight, Carlos closed the gap between them, kissing him. Billy Joe leaned into the kiss, holding a little more tightly, getting lost in both his son and partner. He barely noticed the flash as Angie took their first family picture.

EPILOGUE

"AUNTIE ANGIE is really fat," Tyler said much more loudly than was necessary as Billy Joe hung up with her.

"She's pregnant," Billy Joe corrected as they walked across the college lawn. "She's got a baby inside her, and in a month or so, it will be born and you'll have a little baby girl to get to know." Billy Joe and Carlos had both tried to explain things to him, to no avail. "You were once like that before you were born."

Tyler shook his head violently. "Nope, I'm a big boy, not a belly boy. And I'm not sharing Gramma Sue with no belly girl."

Okay, that needed to be the last word on that subject, because Billy Joe couldn't hold it together for much longer.

Ron and Sue had moved to Shippensburg just a few weeks ago, and already Tyler had finagled two overnights with Gramma Sue and Grampa Ron. Two whole grown-up evenings for Billy Joe and Carlos. He liked to think of those as "naked adult evenings," and they were most appreciated.

"Hi, sweetheart," Sue said as she and Ron approached from the opposite direction. Tyler pulled his hand away and took off at a run. Sue caught him in a hug. "Are you all ready?"

"Yes." Tyler practically shook with excitement. The day care at the college also acted as a preschool, and the kids in Tyler's class were graduating to official pre-K for the fall. Tyler had informed Billy Joe last week that everyone got to wear robes.

"Then let's go. Carlos just called and said he'd be here in a few minutes." Sue took Tyler's hand.

"Angie is on her way too. Apparently she had some twinges this morning in her back, but she's feeling better now." She seemed to get more and more nervous as the pregnancy progressed, which was probably normal.

As they approached the day care center on the edge of campus, Carlos joined them, holding Angie's arm. "I'm so ready to pop out this kid," Angie groaned and wiped the back of her neck with a tissue.

They all went inside. Billy Joe delivered Tyler to his classroom, where the teachers and helpers were getting the kids ready. The excitement was palpable and the noise deafening. Tyler ran to join his friends, and Billy Joe went to the multipurpose room, where chairs had been set up. He stood next to Carlos, who briefly slipped his hand into Billy Joe's.

"The check came today," Carlos whispered. It had taken months, but Carlos's family had sold the land, and he'd been watching for the check, afraid they were going to try to cheat him out of it. "Along with a nasty letter from my cousin." A cloud passed over Carlos's eyes for a second and then went away as quickly as it came. "I put the letter aside and deposited the check with no regret or guilt whatsoever."

"What are you going to do with it?" Sue asked.

"It's in the bank for now, but I think in a year or so, Billy Joe and I will start looking for a house. Part of it can be the down payment. I'd like for Tyler to have a yard where he can play outside, and maybe we'll get him the dog he's been asking for." They were both relieved that the horse had shrunk to a puppy over the past few months. Carlos slipped his arm around Billy Joe's waist, squeezing lightly.

Sue chuckled. "I meant the letter."

"Oh. That I burned. I figured a letter from the devil himself should be sent straight back to hell." Carlos chuckled. "It certainly wasn't worth keeping. I have all the family I need right here." He leaned gently on Billy Joe's shoulder, and Billy Joe leaned right back.

"You two are so adorable," Sue said.

"Yeah, yeah, they're as cute as a litter of puppies." Angie wiped her neck once again, and Sue took her arm. The guys found chairs and sat down. Billy Joe greeted some of the other parents as Angie levered herself into one of the chairs. The poor thing looked like a balloon about ready to pop, but she seemed to get more comfortable once she was down.

Piano music started and expectation jumped as the kids began filing in. They were indeed in blue robes with graduation hats they'd made themselves out of paper. They looked so cute, and Tyler came in, grinning, waving to them as he passed. They waved back as the kids took their places on the small stage. The teacher, a woman in her twenties, Miss Carol, introduced the program, and then the kids all recited a short poem about spring and flowers. Then they sang a song. It was hard to understand the words, but they were enthusiastic. Billy Joe watched Tyler singing and rocking from side to side in sheer happiness. Then the kids filed off to small chairs on the side, and Miss Carol got up once again.

"I'm so happy to see all of you here today. Each of these boys and girls has worked very hard this year. They have learned their numbers and colors, and they know their ABCs. But each of these boys and girls is special. They share with each other and have learned to work together." She turned to the kids. "When I call your name, come up and get your diploma, and then you can go sit with your moms and dads."

"I don't got a mom," Tyler said loud enough for everyone to hear him.

"Then, honey, you go sit with your daddies," Miss Carol said caringly, and Tyler seemed happy. Then she proceeded to call each name, and the little ones filed up, took their scrolls, and raced out to sit with their parents.

When it was Tyler's turn, he took his scroll, hurried to Billy Joe, and jumped into his lap, where Billy Joe hugged him tightly.

"You're getting to be such a big boy," Billy Joe said softly.

"Is it for real now?" Tyler asked, and Billy Joe laughed.

"Yes. It's official." Billy Joe rocked back and forth. His son was growing up. Billy Joe clamped his eyes closed to keep the tears from running down his cheeks. Over the last several months, he liked to think he'd accepted the changes in his life. He had Carlos, who made him happier than Billy Joe could ever think possible. "You're a big boy, and in the fall, you start preschool."

Tyler slipped down and climbed onto Carlos's lap, leaning against him while the rest of the kids got their scrolls. Then Miss Carol told each of them goodbye and the ceremony was over. After standing up, Billy Joe helped Tyler get his robe off, and they hung it up on the rack provided on the way out.

"Billy Joe," Carlos said, pointing to a woman walking toward a car across the way.

Billy Joe paused and nodded, unsure what to do. "Stay here with Tyler." He waited while Carlos held Tyler's hand and then took off toward her. She pulled the car door closed as he approached, so he knocked on the window.

"What are you doing here, Mother?" he asked as she lowered the glass. Billy Joe wondered how she knew about the graduation and where they were, but he could only deal with one thing at a time.

"I just wanted to see him," she said. "He's growing up to look so much like you." She wiped her eyes and leaned forward, holding the steering wheel like it was a lifeline. Billy Joe wasn't buying what she was selling anymore. "What the hell happened to our family?" She lifted her head, wet stripes running down her cheeks. "Your father is gone, prison for the rest of his life most likely. You ran away and took Tyler, and I have nothing."

Billy Joe's resolve faltered, until her gaze hardened and the familiar hate filled her eyes. Billy Joe didn't need to see any more. She wanted only what she wanted, and she might have been willing to come all this way to see Tyler, but her own son wasn't worth the time of day.

"Goodbye, Mom," Billy Joe said and turned away.

"You running away again?" she called after him.

Billy Joe stopped and turned back to her. "No. I'm running toward my family, my real family. The one I built that's filled with people who love me."

He turned away and walked until he ended up in Carlos's arms, magic words whispered into his ear. "I love you."

Then Carlos kissed him.

ANDREW GREY grew up in western Michigan with a father who loved to tell stories and a mother who loved to read them. Since then he has lived all over the country and traveled throughout the world. He has a master's degree from the University of Wisconsin-Milwaukee and now works full-time on his writing. Andrew received the RWA Centennial Award in 2017. His hobbies include collecting antiques, gardening, and leaving his dirty dishes anywhere but in the sink (particularly when writing). He considers himself blessed with an accepting family, fantastic friends, and the world's most supportive and loving husband. Andrew currently lives in beautiful historic Carlisle, Pennsylvania.

Email: andrewgrey@comcast.net
Website: www.andrewgreybooks.com

BURIED PASSIONS

ANDREW GREY

When Broadway actor Jonah receives word that his uncle has passed away and named him the heir to a property in Carlisle, Pennsylvania, Jonah's plan is to settle the estate as quickly as possible and return to his life in New York City. Much to Jonah's surprise, the inheritance includes the Ashford Cemetery—and its hunky groundskeeper, recent Bosnian immigrant Luka Pavelka.

Jonah soon discovers Luka is more than easy on the eyes. He sees into Jonah's heart like no man ever before, and his job at the cemetery is all he has. If Jonah sells, Luka is left with nothing. Luka is there for Jonah when Jonah needs someone most, and there's no denying the chemistry and connection between them. But Jonah has a successful career back in New York. Now he must decide if it's still the life he wants….

www.dreamspinnerpress.com

FIRE *AND* *Flint*

ANDREW GREY

A Carlisle Deputies Novel

Jordan Erichsohn suspects something is rotten about his boss, Judge Crawford. Unfortunately he has nowhere to turn and doubts anyone will believe his claims—least of all the handsome deputy, Pierre Ravelle, who has been assigned to protect the judge after he received threatening letters. The judge has a long reach, and if he finds out Jordan's turned on him, he might impede Jordan adopting his son, Jeremiah.

When Jordan can no longer stay silent, he gathers his courage and tells Pierre what he knows. To his surprise and relief, Pierre believes him, and Jordan finds an ally… and maybe more. Pierre vows to do what it takes to protect Jordan and Jeremiah and see justice done. He's willing to fight for the man he's growing to love and the family he's starting to think of as his own. But Crawford is a powerful and dangerous enemy, and he's not above ripping apart everything Jordan and Pierre are trying to build in order to save himself.…

www.dreanspinnerpress.com

TAMING THE BEAST

ANDREW GREY

The suspicious death of Dante Bartholomew's wife changed him, especially in the eyes of the residents of St. Giles. They no longer see a successful businessman… only a monster they believe was involved. Dante's horrific reputation eclipses the truth to the point that he sees no choice but to isolate himself and his heart.

The plan backfires when he meets counselor Beau Clarity and the children he works with. Beau and the kids see beyond the beastly reputation to the beautiful soul inside Dante, and Dante's cold heart begins to thaw as they slip past his defenses. The warmth and hope Beau brings to Dante's life help him see his entire existence—his trials and sorrows—in a brighter light.

But Dante's secrets could rip happiness from their grasp… especially since someone isn't above hurting those Dante has grown to love in order to bring him down.

www.dreamspinnerpress.com

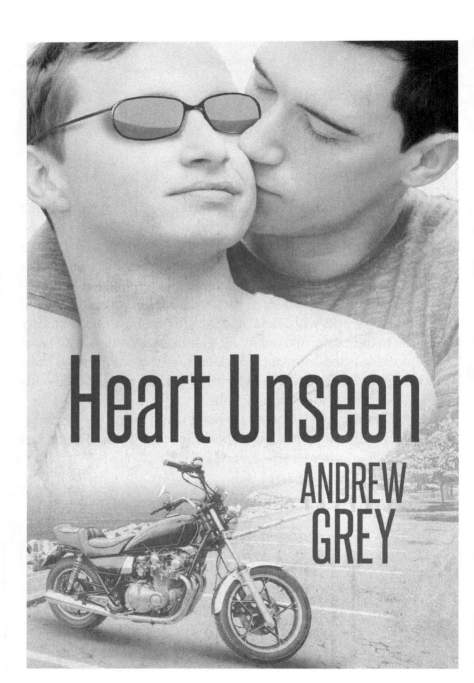

Heart Unseen

ANDREW GREY

A Hearts Entwined Novel

As a stunningly attractive man and the owner of a successful chain of auto repair garages, Trevor is used to attention, adoration, and getting what he wants. What he wants tends to be passionate, no-strings-attached flings with men he meets in clubs. He doesn't expect anything different when he sets his sights on James. Imagine his surprise when the charm that normally brings men to their knees fails to impress. Trevor will need to drop the routine and connect with James on a meaningful level. He starts by offering to take James home instead of James riding home with his intoxicated friend.

For James, losing his sight at a young age meant limited opportunities for social interaction. Spending most of his time working at a school for the blind has left him unfamiliar with Trevor's world, but James has fought hard for his independence, and he knows what he wants. Right now, that means stepping outside his comfort zone and into Trevor's heart.

Trevor is also open to exploring real love and commitment for a change, but before he can be the man James needs him to be, he'll have to deal with the pain of his past.

www.dreamspinnerpress.com

Heart Unheard

ANDREW GREY

A Hearts Entwined Novel

The attraction between Brent Berkheimer and Scott Spearman peels the wallpaper, but Brent is Scott's boss, and they're both too professional to go beyond flirting. Their priorities realign after Scott is badly injured in an accident that costs him his hearing, and Brent realizes what is truly important... he wants Scott.

Scott pushes Brent away at first, fearing a new romance will just add to his problems, but perhaps he will find unexpected strength and solace in Brent's support as he struggles to communicate with the world in a new way.

Just as they decide the chance of a happy future together is worth the risk, Scott and Brent discover darker challenges in their way—including evidence that the "accident" Scott suffered may not have been so accidental.

www.dreamspinnerpress.com

CPSIA information can be obtained
at www.ICGtesting.com
Printed in the USA
BVHW04s1102080818
523842BV00008B/36/P